JEFFREY THOMAS

GODS
OF A
NAMELESS
COUNTRY

ISBN: 978-1-68510-125-1 (sc)
ISBN: 978-1-68510-126-8 (ebook)

"The Children of Lord Ob" first appeared in *The Weird Fiction Review* #11, Centipede Press, 2021.
"Jade Tiger" is original to this collection.
"The First Ones and the Last Ones" is original to this collection.

First printing edition: March 1, 2024
Printed by JournalStone Publishing in the United States of America.
Cover Artwork: Don Noble
Edited by Sean Leonard
Proofreading, Cover Layout, & Interior Layout by Scarlett R. Algee
Author photograph by Colin Thomas

JournalStone Publishing
3205 Sassafras Trail
Carbondale, Illinois 62901

JournalStone books may be ordered through booksellers or by contacting:
or
JournalStone | www.journalstone.com

JOURNALSTONE
YOUR LINK TO ARTIST TALENT

CONTENTS

GODS
OF A
NAMELESS
COUNTRY

THE CHILDREN OF LORD OB

OUT IN FRONT OF the little roadside temple stood a statue of the Ruby Empress, her serene but weather-pitted face runny with black streaks, like makeup diluted by many rains…many a tear, unfathomed by simple mortals. Only the gods comprehended the pain of the gods.

Clutching her shapely legs through their stone robes was her favorite pet, both scribe to the gods and trickster, the Holy Monkey—Cholukan. The only point of variance in this dual sculpture's stone composition was that the devoted macaque Cholukan had red glass orbs seated in his eye sockets, representing the gift of renewed sight bestowed upon him by his beloved Ruby Empress, following his having become blinded for venturing into the realms of Hell—but that was another story.

Well, there *had* been two red orbs, but one of this sculpted Cholukan's glass eyes was missing. No one would dare to remove such a thing, and anyway, unlike an actual ruby, it had no real value. It was more likely that with time and the onslaught of monsoon rains, the small glass sphere had become dislodged naturally, fallen away and rolled off down the forested hillside.

This was, indeed, a very much forested and very hilly area. Mountainous, actually; mountains so steep and continuous that they had aided for many generations in separating and shielding this land—which a long-ago ruler, Emperor Tho, had renamed the Unnamed Country, so as to obscure its existence from the eyes of would-be invaders and would-be troublesome demons—from its neighbor on the other side of the natural wall.

Of course, the "namelessness" of this little country was now just a quaint memento from those ancient times, as tourists these days flew here from the West, and narrow winding roads snaked through these once seemingly impassable wooded mountains, against the slopes of which clouds clung like the slumbering ghosts of dead gods.

The little investigative party had traveled along such serpentine roads, looping higher and higher into the mountains, to arrive at the roadside temple. They had secured a silver van such as tourists would rent when coming to the Unnamed Country, and a driver used to and unafraid of these often vertiginous roads. When he had pulled up in front of the temple, the driver got out of the van to stretch his legs and light a cigarette. It had been an almost five-hour drive here from the capital city of Haikan.

The six passengers that stepped down from the van, once the driver had slid the side panel aside for them, similarly stretched legs and backs, while turning as one to gaze at the temple and the hillside that rose directly behind it.

The party consisted of two police officers—a male captain and a young female subordinate, both in short-sleeved green uniforms with epaulets and a visored green cap—a portly man with a sweat-shiny face who represented the slaughterhouse to which the pigs at the center of this investigation had been bound, a female representative of the Department of Agriculture in Haikan, and a pair of hard-faced, deeply tanned men who carried foreign-made fully automatic assault rifles with long curved magazines. These latter two were usually contracted by the government to hunt other men, typically criminals, who might be trying to escape this country into another illegally.

Guns were hard to come by for average citizens in their country, let alone guns like these, and Veep Sum—from the slaughterhouse's Operations and Management office—wasn't sure if it was these or the small, holstered pistols of the police officers that made him more nervous. It had been a terribly long ride to this place with this group of people, boxed up in the van with the stink of sweat and the CD of foreign pop songs the driver played over and over. Sum had tried to keep himself distracted by chatting quietly with Kwee Ohm, the Department of Agriculture rep, who was soft-spoken and intelligent. He had met her before, briefly, when she had several times been part of an inspection team at the slaughterhouse.

"There's the truck, right there," he said to her now, pointing to a spot between the upper ridge of the hill behind the temple and the temple itself.

"Yes, I saw it," she replied, shielding her eyes with her hand.

"I wonder if the driver dozed off, or if he was drinking," Sum said.

Kwee said, "I don't think we'll find him in a condition to ask him."

The police captain, Zohn, leaned close to the female officer, Laiki, and muttered, "He's been flirting with the livestock expert all day...as if a good-looking woman like her would sleep with a sweaty blob like him. Look at him... He eats so much pork from his slaughterhouse that he looks like a pig himself."

Laiki smiled politely at her superior's joke, but didn't glance over at the two in question. She, too, was looking toward the truck wedged on its side against the trunks of several strong trees, halfway up the precipitous hill.

"Hello!" Captain Zohn called, moving toward the temple now. The others had been waiting for him to put the operation in motion. He strode past the statue of the Ruby Empress at the front of the courtyard, continued between two great urns filled with sand and the pink stubs of hundreds of burnt incense sticks. He paused suddenly, glanced back over his shoulder, and pointed to one of these urns. "Hm!" he said, and Laiki hurried to catch up to him.

"Sir?"

"Do you notice? No new sticks are burning." He lifted his gaze to meet hers. "Are the monks not here?"

"Maybe they heard we were coming," one of the men with the assault rifles said in a voice hard as his face. "Could be they're afraid they're going to get in trouble now, for releasing the pigs."

"We don't know that they did that, until we look at the truck more closely," Kwee spoke up.

"A witness driving past saw two of them up there, cutting through the wire," Zohn replied. "Have we not said that already?"

"They may have been releasing one animal that was snagged," Kwee said. "The others might have all escaped from damage to the cages when the truck went over the side."

"You have seen trucks of this type before, have you not?" Zohn said, his tone becoming more gruff. "How likely is it that all the individual units happened to break open enough to free all those pigs? No, no...I don't know how devout you are, but you mustn't defend these monks' misguided actions. Vegetarians or not, they had no business doing what they did. They should have called us—I'm presuming they have at least one phone in there!—and left the rest to the authorities."

He turned back to the temple, continued walking across the dusty flagstones of the meager courtyard, past a statue of Cholukan's nemesis-turned-friend the Gold-Scaled Dragon, toward the wooden front doors. "Hello!" he shouted again.

Laiki looked back at the statue of the Ruby Empress. The yellow flowers in two vases set at its base had wilted, and the rotten fruit offered in a bowl between them was swarming with ants. She looked back toward the temple and resumed following after the captain.

The temple was smallish, of course, apparently with only two floors, its three tiers of tiled roof curled up sharply at every corner, its outer walls going blackish with mildew. A humble place indeed, but travelers through here would stop to say a prayer for luck, if native to the country, or snap photos for social media if from the West. Often, Western women would copy the dignified pose of the Empress, while their man would clutch at her legs comically like the Holy Monkey.

"Hey!" one of the hired hunters cried, whirling around to point his weapon toward the thick trees that bordered the temple grounds on the right. Though this was a tropical country, at this high elevation the air was cooler and the trees tended to be sturdy pines.

"What is it?" his fellow hunter said, aiming his own assault rifle in that direction.

His friend didn't answer at first, staring into the woods warily.

"Did you see something?" Veep Sum, the slaughterhouse man, said.

"Shh!"

"Be careful!" Kwee Ohm warned, holding up a hand. "It could be one of the monks…or a child playing in the trees, don't forget!"

The first hunter snarled. "Do you think I don't know the difference between a pig and a child?"

Zohn and Laiki had stopped advancing on the temple to look back and watch the hunters. The first man finally lowered his rifle a bit but stalked forward toward the trees. He didn't have to say anything to his partner or even gesture to indicate he should stay back and protect the others. He stepped into the underbrush, and into shadow, and was gone from sight.

"Are the pigs really that dangerous?" Laiki whispered to Zohn.

"You don't know pigs, huh?" Zohn said. "Remember, it's been three weeks since the accident. This place is so remote, we didn't know where the truck went missing until a tourist stopping here spotted it and made a call. Who can tell how many others saw it up there but didn't care enough to report it. Anyway…ask our livestock expert over there, and she'll tell you: domestic pigs returned to the wild can become feral swine in no time. In just months, they adapt…their bodies get hairy, their tusks grow longer. They get mean…they'll eat anything, and not just crops. I've heard of them killing and eating baby deer."

Laiki looked at her superior. She saw he had his hand on the butt of his holstered pistol as he stared off in the direction the hunter had disappeared.

"You, slaughterhouse man!" he said. Sum snapped his head around. "Climb up there and examine that truck. See if you can determine the cause of the accident. See if there's a body in there."

Sum's face was the definition of surprise, a portrait of distress. "But...sir...isn't that your realm of expertise?"

"I'm just asking you to make a preliminary examination! Can't you see I'm busy here? The truck and its driver belonged to your company!"

"Yes, sir...of course."

"Take pictures. I'll go over them soon enough. I'm sure you'll see that the cages were cut into, not burst open."

Sum looked up the wooded cliff dubiously. "Uh...yes...pictures."

"If those old monks could get up there, you can do it."

"I'll go with you," Kwee said to Sum.

Zohn redirected his attention to the temple doors, and when he reached them he found them locked. He pounded the heel of his fist on the wood. "You in there! Open up! Police...official business!"

"I hear music inside," Laiki said, putting her ear to the other panel of the double doors. "A recording of chants and gongs."

"They're in there then," Zohn said, smiling without charm. "Hiding. Do they think their religion makes them exempt from the law?" He thumped the door again. *"Hey!"*

* * *

Sum huffed as he worked his way up a narrow path from the rear of the temple toward where the slaughterhouse company's truck was jammed into the gaps between pine trunks. He grabbed at branches or fistfuls of bushes occasionally to help him past precarious points. Kwee climbed behind him. At last, they reached the old truck. There were three levels of cages. Even empty, they stank.

"Not a single dead body," Kwee observed.

Sum whipped his head around. At first he had thought she meant there was no dead driver in the cab. Or...had she meant that? Because no one had heard from the driver since the accident had occurred some weeks back.

"These cages were cut," she admitted, fingering the clean ends of black wire encrusted with years of filth. "You see? So the monks did free them."

"But as you say, no dead bodies. Did every pig survive the wreck and get away into the forest?"

"If any of them died, I suspect the monks in their compassion would have removed them and buried them. The driver too."

"No, no, no... They wouldn't take it upon themselves to bury the driver, would they? Surely they would have called the police in the nearest town or something."

"Well…he isn't here," Kwee said, leaning over the side of the cab to look through its open driver's-side window. The windshield was bowed inward and webbed with cracks, but had still held together in one piece. She was taking pictures of all this with her cell phone, on Sum's behalf.

"Do you think locals might have captured some of the pigs, to keep for themselves?" Sum said, looking out upon the countryside from their elevated vantage point. From here, though, he saw no towns in the distance, unless small villages lurked here and there beneath all those green treetops. Only the slender road threaded between the mountains, with sheets of mist along their flanks like slow-motion avalanches of snow.

"Maybe…some," Kwee said. "They would be difficult to catch though, I imagine. You know what breed they are. Ob pigs. They were bred to be big, and they're strong—and aggressive even at the best of times. But smart…very smart. Pigs are smart anyway—the seventh smartest type of animal."

"I've heard that. Smarter than dogs."

"Probably smarter than that stupid police captain pounding on the doors down there."

Sum chuckled. "Yes, the Ob breed is even smarter than normal. A perhaps unintended development of animal husbandry…but you know all about that in your field."

"I've heard that pigs can be trained to play some video games."

"*What?* Even I can't play video games."

Kwee fingered another rough end of snipped wire. "I hate the way they pack the animals into these cages. Until their flesh bulges out the sides. Sometimes they're pressed together so tightly their guts pop out their backsides. Many arrive at their destination unable to walk…and the slaughterhouse workers beat them for it."

"Oh no, no… At my company we have strict guidelines about unnecessary cruelty! And I dislike that they overpack these trucks myself. I've made my feelings known about that, on multiple occasions!"

Kwee looked at his perspiring face. He dropped his gaze, unable to uphold the lie. After a thoughtful moment, Kwee said, "I remember being shown an animated film when I was a child, to frighten me about being punished for sins by the Ten Demon Lords of Hell. I remember that one of the punishments was for the sin of eating meat without first thanking the soul of the slain animal. The punishment was to be reincarnated as a pig, so ill that it can't even feed and it starves to death in agony. I remember I had a nightmare once about that, where I dreamed I was a pig…emaciated, nothing but bones, too weak to rise from its corner. I woke up screaming…my parents came running in, and—"

"Hey," Sum said, gripping her shoulder, pointing into the truck's cab.

Kwee looked. She leaned in closer than she had previously, thrusting her head through the open driver's-side window.

"Is that…" she said. "Is that blood?"

* * *

"I'm no hunter, but…" the driver called over to the police officers, as he stood smoking at one edge of the courtyard, where the flagstones gave way to a strip of bare dirt before that was lost to the forest. He pointed down near his shoes. He was careful not to step on and mar what he indicated.

Having no luck at the doors, the captain approached him to see what the man had discovered. Laiki too.

"Huh," said Zohn. "Yes, of course. Ob pig tracks. See the little 'thumb,' as they call it?"

Laiki had never seen prints left by pigs before, or at least had never had cause to notice them, but she had of course seen severed Ob trotters in markets and restaurants many a time. Who hadn't? As a consequence of directed breeding, the twisting of nature, a mutation had become the norm. Instead of just the two major toes and two lesser dewclaws of a regular pig's foot, Ob pigs had an additional longer dewclaw off to one side on their front feet…on the inside of the foot, hence their being called "thumbs."

"Lots of prints, overlapping each other," Laiki observed.

"Of course," said Zohn. "They milled about here for a bit before scattering into the forest."

Gunfire.

Deep in the woods—it was hard for any of them, except perhaps the other hunter, to gauge the distance. It was a short, fully automatic burst. Laiki thought that was odd, brash—surely a waste of ammunition.

The other hunter looked sharply over to the two police officers, mutely asking for permission. One could see his anxiousness to charge into the forest from his tense pose.

"Yes, go!" Zohn called. He drew his sidearm. "I have it covered here!"

Following his lead, Laiki withdrew her own semiautomatic pistol, and saw the second hunter plunge into the woods.

"How many of them are there again? From the truck?" she asked Zohn.

"I believe they said about a hundred."

Laiki nodded slowly, absorbing this fact. Their mission was to investigate the crash, the reason for the escape of the pigs, and to exterminate any they discovered until a follow-up expedition might try to recapture those they could and transport them along to the slaughterhouse that had been awaiting this cargo…but it all seemed so unrealistic to her now, beyond the cursory investigation itself. She supposed the whole operation at this point was merely a formality, a gesture, like so much of police and government business.

"Damn these stubborn old monks," Zohn said. "Come on, let's look around for another way inside."

*　　*　　*

"Oh no, ohhh," said Sum, looking out into all that wild greenery. He saw nothing but the greenery. "They must have found one of them. Maybe more."

"I hope it's that," Kwee said, "and not some poor innocent person."

"They know what they're doing…but we should really get down there and join the rest. I wouldn't want to encounter some feral pig without a gun, would you? Do you have enough pictures? I think we've established what happened here."

"I think we have enough photos." Kwee had captured digital images, too, of the old, blackish blood stains that had splattered across and run down the cushions of the passenger's seat.

Sum led the way again, once more grabbing whatever handhold he could to ease himself down the insufficient trail. He nearly fell back onto his rear at one point, but Kwee lunged forward to prop him up.

Just as they reached level ground again, they heard the driver call from the front of the temple, "Hey!"

Along one side of the temple, Kwee and Sum encountered Zohn and Laiki, peeking through a narrow pillbox-style window without glass, unable as yet to find another way inside. The four of them returned to the courtyard together, and there found the driver pointing toward the building's heavy wooden double doors. The one on the right stood open a crack. His cigarette bobbed in his mouth as he explained, "I just saw it open."

"I guess we scared them enough," Zohn said, striding forward triumphantly. He shoved the door open wider.

Within the temple it was gloomy, the air packed solid with heat and an unbearable stench…worse than what Kwee had encountered at the truck.

A floor fan had toppled and lay on its side, not operating. Without thinking, with one hand clamped over her nose and mouth, Kwee stooped down to right the fan. A drone of monks chanting, laid over the hum of singing bowls and punctuated with the gong of standing bells, played softly from a speaker mounted high on one wall of this largish main room with its glossy tiled floor. At the far end of the room: an elaborate shrine dominated by gold-painted figures representing the Ten Jeweled Gods. The only artificial light in here came from strings of small colored bulbs worked into and bordering parts of the shrine. Again, joss sticks had burned down to a stubble in urns, flowers drooped in vases. And in the center of the floor was arranged a tight circle of dead bodies, rotting in the heat.

"Insane," hissed Captain Zohn behind the hand that cupped his own face. "Why would they do this?"

At first, in the room's murk, Laiki had taken these bodies to be the monks themselves. It was tradition, she knew well from having visited many a temple in her life, for monks to pray in a circle, bowing down low, though this act was usually centered around a graven image, an idol such as a statue of one of the Ten Jeweled Gods. But there was nothing at the center of this circle of humped bodies, and these were not human monks but decomposing pigs. It looked as though they were deflating, collapsing into themselves. Bones showed in places through drying, blackening hides.

For her part, Kwee was reminded of her nightmare of many years ago, and the heat and the stink made her lightheaded. She had to control herself from dashing back outside into the courtyard to vomit.

"The monks must have been praying over them," the driver said. He didn't cover his mouth; the smoke of his cigarette helped sufficiently in masking the foulness for him.

"Insanity," the police captain repeated. "So they've kept these here for, what, three weeks or so? Instead of burying them? Do they *like* this smell?"

"There are only supposed to be three monks here," Laiki said. "They're all old...maybe they're senile."

"They have some answering to do," Zohn said, looking about for stairs or doorways that would communicate with other areas of the building. He spotted a darkened doorway, skirted around the circle of perhaps a dozen dead pigs to reach it. As always, Laiki diligently trailed him. They both hadn't yet put their handguns away. Laiki looked down at the pigs as she passed them, and now made out smudges of dried blood across the tiles from where the bodies had been dragged. In fact, she realized the floor was smeared and pooled with caked and flaking old blood everywhere. She had at first taken all this to be some sort of design in the tiles.

Beyond the decomposition of the animals, she also noted signs of violence: a missing limb here, a crushed skull there. She took these to be animals that had died directly as a result of the crash. She might have thought, presented in this circle so ritualistically, that they had been arranged here as an offering to the Ten Jeweled Gods...if she wasn't aware that it was forbidden to gift them with offerings of meat. She herself was devout enough that she was a vegetarian.

"Oh!" Sum exclaimed, raising his arm to point, but the others had already heard the snuffling sound from one of the pillbox windows without glass spaced evenly about the room.

A face, dark and silhouetted, had appeared there. The window was too narrow for even a head to push through, so mostly it was just eyes—reflecting multicolored sparks from the shrine's decorative bulbs—that showed in the slit.

The snorting gave it away for what it was though. One of the pigs... But how could it reach that window to peer in at them, Kwee wondered, unless the thing were standing on two legs?

It must be bracing its front hooves against the wall, she thought. *Must be.*

A horrible image flashed into her mind. As a child, she had visited a major temple in Haikan on a class trip, and their trip had culminated with the schoolgirls venturing into what was essentially a ghost train attraction beneath it. Narrow, winding dark tunnels with faux rock walls of plaster over chicken wire, opening at every bend upon a scene of hellish suffering. There were no humans turned to starving pigs here, but so many images of suffering far worse as sinners were tortured and tormented in a variety of imaginative ways. At last, the children were brought before brightly painted effigies of the Ten Demon Lords of Hell. A recording played of the demons presiding over a court to determine whether these visitors should be allowed to return to the land of the living or not. Well, of course the doors to the exit were opened to allow the admonished visitors to depart, but with terrible imagery forever seared into their minds.

That night, alone in her bedroom, young Kwee had wept quietly and offered up a string of repeated prayers remembered from her teachings. She had chanted, "Oh merciful Ruby Empress, who healed her beloved Holy Monkey, Cholukan, from the woundings of Hell...I beseech you to protect me from that realm and all its demons. I vow my loyalty to you...I promise to cleanse my soul and avoid all sin. Please, oh merciful Ruby Empress!"

Kwee would never forget the faces of the Ten Demon Lords, the most horrifying, of course, being that of the cyclops-like Tenth Lord. The demon she thought of now, however, was Ob—for whom this breed of pig was named—his muscular anthropomorphic body topped with the shaggy head of a boar. Great tusks curved up from his scowling mouth, and the effigy's eyes were bulbs that glowed a furious red.

A sound like a thunderbolt striking the temple caused Kwee to jolt and gasp so harshly that her lungs filled with the room's miasma even through her fingers.

Captain Zohn had jumped forward, pistol extended, like a swordsman plunging his blade into an enemy's heart, and fired one shot at the window. He struck the edge of it, but fragments of plaster and maybe of bullet sprayed the pig in the eyes. With a squeal, the head dropped out of view, and even from in here—even with their ears ringing—they could hear the animal crashing through the underbrush.

"Captain!" Kwee cried. "How can you fire a weapon inside this holy place?"

"This is no time for superstitions," Zohn snapped. He was clearly a man devoted only to his mortal office, rather than that of the gods. "These are Ob pigs gone feral! They pose a danger to anyone who might encounter them! They could breed out here in these woods, breed hordes of them before we can—"

His words were cut off by a prolonged rattle of automatic gunfire out there in the woods somewhere. This was followed, from perhaps further beyond, by a similar burst of fire. The two guns answered back and forth, and one might have wondered if some old enmity between the rough-faced hunters had erupted and they were finally settling it with murderous intent. But one of the guns went silent at last, and the other rattled off another burst after that until it went dry. They all stood poised, their ringing ears cocked for more gunfire...perhaps a cry for help or scream of pain. But nothing more.

"Come back here," Sum whispered. "Be alive. Come back."

"I don't think they're coming back," said the driver, stubbing out the butt of his cigarette and tucking it in the pocket of his shorts, rather than disrespectfully littering the temple's floor. This blood-smeared floor with its circle of fermenting pig carcasses. Multitudes of flies crawled over the corpses in living tattoos, briefly took to flight from one to another as if the other might be more delightfully foul.

"They're manhunters," Zohn said. "They'll come back dragging one of those brutes. Two of them!"

"These aren't men," said the driver.

"Exactly! Men are more clever. More dangerous!"

"Maybe," Kwee said to herself. "And maybe."

"They're not coming back," the driver insisted. "Come on...we need to get in the van and get out of here."

"What are you saying?" Zohn growled. "We aren't leaving those men...and those monks let us in here! They're hiding upstairs. You go sit in your van if you're afraid. Laiki, with me! Upstairs!"

"Yes, sir." She was glad at least for being able to move away from the O of carcasses.

Behind them, a humped shape, shaggy as if darkness clung to it in tatters, plummeted through the opened half of the double doors.

Zohn looked back, wheeled with his handgun, fired once and missed...couldn't fire a second time because the pig was on top of the driver, who had been standing nearest to the doors. It had butted him in the back, knocking him off his feet, and then it was goring him, getting him up under the chin, flipping its massive head from side to side to alternate its tusks. The driver was screaming and trying to scramble away on all fours as fresh blood poured from his gashed throat to paint new patterns atop the old on the tiles.

Laiki was closer to the pig than Zohn, and she lunged forward and fired two rounds into its hindquarters. The animal squealed, swung its head her way, maddened whites showing around its tiny black eyes. The driver went flat on his face, heaving with wet gurgles. Zohn had a clear shot now, and before the pig could charge Laiki he fired three times at its head. Even still, she had to jump to one side to avoid its forward momentum before it crashed to the floor, kicked crazily, then went still.

Kwee crouched down beside the driver. He was making slow, sweeping movements with his limbs as if trying to swim through his own blood. No longer gurgling.

"Laiki," Zohn shouted over the ringing of remembered gunfire, "bolt the doors!"

She moved to the wooden panels, and as she began pushing shut the open door she saw two pigs out there, dashing from the boundary of the forest. And more behind them, back in the trees. She got the door closed, shoved a heavy bolt into place. Normally, temples did not lock or bar their doors—all souls in need of solace, all those who sought to offer respect to the gods, should be welcome at any time—but out here in the mountains, on the periphery of the Unnamed Country where foreign enemies had once stubbornly trickled across the border, precautions had formerly needed to be taken.

Laiki backed up wildly as the door jolted with a heavy impact. A second tremendous thud. They were dashing their very skulls against the thick wood.

"He's dead," Kwee said, looking up at Zohn, tears shivering in her eyes. She didn't care about sucking in the room's stench anymore, accidentally ingesting one of the swarming flies. "It tore open his carotid artery."

"Bastards!" Zohn yelled. Then he looked up at the ceiling and shouted again, the same word for other enemies. "Bastards!"

"Oh dear oh dear oh dear," Sum was moaning, staring at the driver's motionless body in its spreading pool of blood, covering his ears with both hands as if to drown out his own voice. "Oh dear oh dear…"

Kwee backed away from the body, stood beside Sum, switched her horrified gaze to the dead pig as if afraid it would spring up…not really dead.

Laiki stood on tiptoes, peeking out one of the slot-like windows. "I see more out there, running all around the building."

"They want to eat us!" Sum groaned. "They've probably exhausted all the small game around here… They'll eat that, you know? Birds, lizards, rabbits, young livestock. They've got us trapped!"

"Sir," Laiki said to her boss, "we need to call this in and have help come meet us."

"In a minute," he said, leaving his cell phone pocketed, once more heading for that dark doorway at the far end of the room. This time, finally, he reached it…stepped through. He called back, his voice echoing, "I'm going to make those monks sorry they didn't live the life of sinners!"

Multiple heads still pounded at the front doors like battering rams, taking turns. And then, abruptly, the hammering stopped. They all paused, Laiki in the threshold of the doorway through which the captain had passed. A moment later, one of the handles of the double doors rattled. Rattled again.

"Oh dear!" Sum hissed.

"Is that someone out there?" Kwee whispered. *The missing hunters?*

"It's them," Sum whined. "It's *them!*"

Laiki whirled to see eyes peering in at them through one of the window slits. *There*…and there too, at a window on the other side of the room!

"*Oh!*" the three on the ground floor heard Zohn cry out upstairs. "*Ohhh!*"

Laiki was through the doorway, pouncing onto a flight of stairs, pounding up them. Pistol still gripped in her fist.

Sum and Kwee followed after more reluctantly, half hanging back.

At the top of the stairs, Zohn partly blocked the doorway, so Laiki pushed past him, and then saw the four human corpses on the floor directly before them.

The monks had their quarters up here, under this low roof made lower by its heavy dark rafters. Narrow cots were pushed up against the walls. There was an area for the preparation of food, including a small electric stove atop a crude counter. One of the two curtained doorways probably gave access to a bathroom. The center of the wooden floor was mostly an open space, and it was here that what was left of the bodies had been arranged in a circle, face down, as if the four men had prostrated themselves in worship. Heads pointing inward, legs splayed at the outside of the circle like the rays of a star. In addition to the rot of time, the little flesh that remained boiling with maggots, they had been ravaged. A few limbs had come detached in the process, and one head, but they had been prodded close enough to the bodies to give the appearance of being still connected. Three of the bodies still bore the ragged remnants of sapphire blue robes, the traditional garb of monks, and their heads had been shaved, but the fourth corpse appeared to be in common street clothes, and he still had a few tufts of hair left on his otherwise stripped and shattered skull.

"The truck driver," Laiki murmured.

"Ohhh…oh dear," Sum said, looking sharply away. "They ate them. *Look* at them! They *ate* them!"

"They put them here like this," Kwee said. "The pigs."

"Why?" asked Laiki, stricken. Fascinated.

"They did eat them…but they paid them a respect. For saving them from the cages. For cutting them free."

"But how did they know to do that?"

"Maybe they saw the monks praying this way downstairs."

"They probably saw the monks arrange the pigs downstairs like this."

"No," said Zohn, understanding now. "The monks didn't arrange the dead pigs that way. The other swine did it."

"But why?" Laiki persisted.

"Because they're demons," he said. "They did it to mock this holy place."

"I don't think so," Kwee said.

"Hey," said Sum, jerking up his head suddenly.

"So you know the minds of pigs?" Zohn shouted at Kwee. "You know that a herd of dumb animals put the bodies of their fellows down there, and the monks up here, to pay *tribute* to them?"

"*Hey!*" Sum repeated.

Zohn bulged his eyes at him. "*What?*"

Sum said, "The front door was bolted when we came, remember? So who unlocked it to let us inside?"

Zohn's eyebrows shot up under his cap's visor. "Ho!"

Sum went on, "Do you see? They let us inside to *trap* us in here!"

A tremendous crash downstairs, involving the splintering of wood. The front doors? Or, having been distracted from fully circumnavigating the temple, had they overlooked some less sturdy side door? In any case, the crash was followed by the sound of numerous five-toed hooves on tile…and a mixture of snorting, grunting, and grumbling that sounded like the ominous voices of a vengeful mob.

"They're in!" Sum shrieked, seizing onto Kwee's arm. "They're in!"

The curtains to both of the adjacent second-floor rooms were wrenched aside, torn away, and a figure appeared in both doorways. They were hulking, bristling with newly sprouted hair, with eyes that—while black—seemed to blaze with fire. Both figures stood upright upon their hind legs.

Then they were throwing themselves forward, and one of them collided with Zohn before he could trigger his pistol. It flew from his hand. The pig dropped to all fours and flipped the police captain's loose-limbed body up over its back. It had purposely gored him in the inner thigh. He flopped to the floor, rolled a few times, screaming and trying to grasp his torn leg tightly enough to stop the gushing from his severed femoral artery.

The other pig had reached Sum, and they, too, went to the floor together. The reverent circle of corpses was disturbed; that one detached skull went rolling. Kwee turned away to retrieve Zohn's handgun, but from the corner of her eye saw the chaos of movement as the pig savaged Sum. She made out flashes of detail as she spun around and pointed the gun in both hands—a tusk fully imbedded in one of Sum's eye sockets, his other eye staring at her, twitching a little—and then she started shooting the pig again and again through the neck, hoping to strike its spine. It reared up on its hind legs to face her, its tusk ripping free from Sum, but she put the last of the bullets through its chest and it only staggered a few steps toward her before thumping heavily onto its belly, lifeless.

Kwee had been aware of other gun blasts overlapping her own. She looked to see Laiki there, still pointing her service gun at the other pig though it had fallen onto its side and heaved with dying breaths. Zohn had managed to drag himself into a corner, half shielded by a cot, where he still gripped his thigh with slick, weakening fingers. His face had gone white, his mouth hung slack, and his eyes might have been the only part of him still alive.

The dying pig raised its head and rolled one eye to look up at Laiki. It made some guttural sound. It was almost like a word, but how could it be? And then the head dropped and the eye seemed to glaze over. Moments later, so did Zohn's.

Laiki switched out the magazine in her gun, adding a fresh one. She and Kwee listened to all the hooves downstairs...all that ominous grumbling.

The bottom stairs creaked.

Laiki turned to see Kwee lowering herself to sit on the edge of one of the monks' cots. The young officer smiled bravely, but her eyes were filling up. She pulled the gun's slide to chamber the first round. "I don't want to be torn apart. Eaten alive."

"Me first," Kwee whispered. "Then you."

Still smiling, Laiki said, "Okay."

More creaking from more bodies easing themselves up the staircase, horribly stealthy.

"But wait...just a moment," Kwee said.

"Hurry."

Kwee closed her eyes and recited a prayer remembered from childhood. After only a few words of it, Laiki recognized the prayer and joined in, and they completed it together.

They said, "Oh merciful Ruby Empress, who healed her beloved Holy Monkey, Cholukan, from the woundings of Hell...I beseech you to protect me from that realm and all its demons. I vow my loyalty to you...I promise to cleanse my soul and avoid all sin. Please, oh merciful Ruby Empress!"

JADE TIGER

-Part 1-

ONE OF THE JADE tigers, a nearly adult male, had risen to its feet and was currently making a series of strange little cries that imitated the sounds a langur monkey would make in calling to its kind. The cries were higher in pitch than one would expect a tiger capable of, but Jhan knew that this clever tiger had learned to imitate these sounds while still a cub in the wild, and used them not to lure prey—as was usually the case with such imitation—but to garner more attention from its mother than its fellow cubs.

Those siblings might be in this very room, in other enclosures, or perhaps already dead and processed by now. He lost track sometimes of which were which.

Jhan wondered why this particular tiger—without a name, just like the rest—chose to make these cries. Did it still hope even now for its mother to come to its aid, or was it simply out of boredom?

The jade tiger was a subspecies indigenous only to the Unnamed Country, and it was estimated that only twenty or thirty of them still lived in the wild, but there were seventeen of them currently in the basement of Uncle Zep's house, in barred cells lining a narrow hallway, ten cells to a side, several empty. The basement was full of the cats' musky, pungent scent, with its hint of meat decaying in their teeth, and the smell of their urine (because they of course urinated in their cells, which Jhan hosed clean often) reminding Jhan oddly of the scent of buttered popcorn.

Jhan had already seen to the feeding of the tigers that day, throwing slabs of raw meat up over the high barred walls. The meat had come from an ox Uncle Zep had purchased in town at the cattle market. It had been bought for a decent price, probably because the animal had lacked a tail. The seller had claimed a pack of wild dogs had attacked the ox and torn its tail off in the process, but Jhan strongly suspected the animal had been born with a white tail, and so the owner had chopped the tail off himself and discarded it. Oxen with white tails were considered not just unlucky, but possible harbingers of doom. This hadn't seemed to trouble Uncle Zep though, with his seventeen big cats to feed.

"Hey!" Jhan said to the noisy cat through its bars, in the language of his people, the citizens of the Unnamed Country. "What's your problem, huh?"

At his voice, the great cat quit its strange vocalizations and turned its head to look out at him, as if roused from a weird reverie, its eyes showing through the spaces between the bars. The shadows of those bars lay across the male's head and body like manmade additions to its own pattern of narrow stripes. Its true stripes were black, on a field of fur that was yellowish-green in hue, like the color of moss. This greenish color was not really like the typical color of jade, but these unique tigers, known only to the isolated Unnamed Country, were called jade tigers nonetheless. Jhan thought this green color must surely make them the best camouflaged of all tigers, but they were on the smaller side compared to some types, adults ranging between three hundred and four hundred pounds.

Behind him, Jhan heard a deep lowing call, then another. He turned toward the sound. "Hey!" he said in the commanding, superior tone of voice he used to talk to the cats. It wasn't a voice he used with any human, certainly not Uncle Zep or Aunt Choit. "Now what is it with you?"

This other tiger had also risen to its heavy paws, instead of lying upon the cement floor as they usually did, and begun imitating the sounds of that tailless ox his uncle's man Lhop had butchered the other day. Jhan wasn't all that familiar with the sound of langur monkeys, but he could easily have believed it was an actual ox making those utterances behind him. He recalled that two years ago his uncle had owned a tiger that made sounds in imitation of motorbikes as they buzzed past in the dirt road in front of the house. The tiger's imitation would start faint, like a motorbike approaching, peak, then fade, like the bike continuing on into the distance. That tricky creature had long ago been turned to bone glue.

"Hey!" Jhan said to this other tiger, a female, who mooed again, looking off in another direction as if willfully ignoring him. "Are you two in some kind of competition with each other?"

"Don't you worry about that one taunting you," came a voice behind Jhan, and he started. He hadn't heard his Aunt Choit enter the basement. Though she always moved with a kind of shambling walk, she did so with such stealthy quiet it put these predators to shame. In turning, he saw his aunt was gesturing toward the young male. "Your uncle is taking him into the forest soon enough."

"Oh, Auntie?" Jhan said.

"Yes. Your uncle has a new client. He's going into Haikan to make arrangements with him tomorrow, in fact." She nudged Jhan out of her way roughly to get past him in the narrow walkway between cells. Jhan moved aside for her, saying nothing, but grateful he hadn't lost his balance and fallen against the bars of the cage of that big female lowing like an ox. Aunt Choit continued explaining as she passed, "He's going to take you with him. It's time you learned how these transactions are done."

His aunt stopped in front of the last cage on the right, in which an emaciated tiger lay on its side, panting through open jaws, staring into a corner of its cell that was black with mildew as if the shadows had coagulated there. "Hey!" she snapped at this animal, holding out a gob of meat, flopping it in her hand. Jhan knew that the meat had been injected with medicine, since this tiger was clearly seriously ill and failing. "Hey, you! Get up and eat this!"

"It can't get up anymore, Auntie," Jhan said timidly. He was more afraid of his aunt than he was of the cats. "I haven't seen him get up in days."

His aunt swore colorfully in their language and took up a metal spear that leaned against the wall at the end of the hallway. Jhan had seen Lhop kill tigers and oxen both with that spear. Aunt Choit stuck the gob of meat onto its end, then extended the spear between the bars. "Hey!" she said to the sick cat. "Hey, you pathetic sack of bones! Don't you see this? Do you *want* to die?"

The cat seemed to roll its eye in the direction of the hovering spear, but it didn't so much as raise its great head—the only thing that was still great about it—not even when Aunt Choit poked the cat's jaw. Swearing again as she manipulated the spear growing heavier in her hands, she managed to scrape the piece of meat along a lower fang and off the spear tip, into the tiger's mouth. It made some gagging motions as it gulped the morsel down.

"Oh yes," Aunt Choit said, "this one is headed for the pot soon enough… Very soon. Your lazy uncle should get to it, or the thing will die before he can kill it and start to rot. It's in much too terrible shape for that new client of his…much too terrible for a good client like him. He needs something young and strong."

"He'd make a good breeder though," Jhan suggested, jerking a thumb toward the cat who had imitated a monkey. It no longer made those sounds, but remained standing, watching through the bars, as if listening in on their conversation.

Aunt Choit turned slowly, gaze menacing, spear in hands, as if she intended to thrust it forward into Jhan's neck. "So are you telling us our business now? Do you think you know better than us?"

"No, Auntie…I'm sorry!"

"We have other breeders. I just told you…this new client is important. You'll see for yourself tomorrow."

To his relief, Aunt Choit leaned the spear back in its spot.

*   *   *

Though not tall, Uncle Zep's man Lhop was solidly built, like one of the bears of the type that had done that to his face. Lhop wore a plastic nose of a pale color that didn't match his skin tone, with a thick fake mustache attached to its bottom to hide the fact that he had no upper lip. Uncle Zep had joked to Jhan that it wasn't a bear that had taken off part of Lhop's face, but a jealous husband, because Lhop had put his nose where it didn't belong. He'd joked this in a whisper though, because however loyal of an employee Lhop was, he was not the type of man to mock to his face…or what he had left of a face.

Lhop had retired from working as an independent hunter after that incident, and instead of supplying bear parts and other materials to various sellers and apothecaries, gone to work for Uncle Zep's tiger farm.

Lhop would drive Uncle Zep and Jhan to the capital city of Haikan today—a good six-hour trip even without stops—but he would then stay at the hotel where they'd be spending the night before their return, since he was too recognizable to be seen with. Uncle Zep's enterprise was against the law, after all, and criminals in the Unnamed Country faced serious jail time in seriously uncomfortable prisons, if not the firing squad. Still, one did what one had to do to survive…just like the animals in the deep of the jungle.

While Lhop went to bring his miniature box truck around to the front of Uncle Zep's house, which stood surrounded by banana trees here in a very much rural area of the Unnamed Country, Jhan decided to steal a couple minutes to seek out his cousin, Mi. Mi was eighteen to Jhan's nineteen, as quiet a young woman as the girl he had met when he'd first come to live with his uncle to learn a trade, so that he might send money home to his struggling parents in their small village up in the mountains. As he had hoped, he found Mi alone in a large shed of corrugated metal out behind the house, which they kept padlocked on the inside at night. Here, she was currently monitoring the boiling down of tiger bones in a sixty-liter pressure cooker that rested upon a four-burner portable gas stove, the propane tank for which she had just switched out. On the floor were plastic tubs of broken tiger bones of various types that would be fed into the cooker in gradual batches. It took between two to three days to boil bones down into the viscous sludge called bone glue. This concentrated sap-like material would be sold in simply labeled bottles to clients, who would add the medicinal glue to rice wine to be taken in small daily portions.

In a refrigerator in a corner were stacked packages of tiger meat, and tiger penises to be made into soup. They didn't keep tiger skins out here in the shed, however, though every night Lhop slept in a curtained-off corner with a black-market military rifle under his bunk. As valuable as the rest of these materials were, intact skins were far too expensive to keep around. Too tempting for thieves too lazy to hunt or capture jade tigers themselves. Anyway, the green-furred tiger skins always sold quickly, as there was a waiting list.

Standing by the pressure cooker, Mi wore a cloth mask over the lower half of her pretty face. Above that mask, her eyes looked alarmed to see Jhan appear at the shed's open door. She was no doubt afraid her mother would catch them alone together, as when Aunt Choit had caught them two years ago, in what Jhan had thought was a private enough spot in which to experiment with kissing for the first time for the both of them. Aunt Choit had tugged down Jhan's pants and placed a knife blade behind his scrotum, reminding him that he was her daughter's cousin. After making this point, she had turned and held Mi by the hair with her free hand, the other laying the knife blade flat upon Mi's flushed cheek, and reminded Mi that Jhan was her cousin, and if she ever let him put his dirty hands on her again she'd feed Mi to the tigers, daughter or no. Bit by bit, just like they fed the bones of the tigers Lhop butchered into the pressure cooker.

"I'm going to Haikan today," Jhan said to Mi.

"I know, Mommy told me."

"Okay." Jhan nodded, not knowing what else to say for small talk. Then inspiration struck. "If I can buy something for you while I'm there, is there anything you'd like me to get...if I can? If Uncle lets me have a little time, since we're spending the night?"

"Better not," she said.

"Oh," Jhan said. "Well...okay."

"I'd better get back to work," Mi said. "And you'd better go."

"Yeah," Jhan said dejectedly. He started to turn away. Anyway, he could hear the rickety old truck rattling along out front.

"I hate this," Mi said behind him.

Jhan turned, looking back into the gloomy shed, shielding his face from the glare through the banana leaves. "What do you hate, Mi?"

"This." She inclined her head toward the foul-smelling basins of bones near her feet. "Imprisoning these beautiful wild cats. Slaughtering them. Boiling them down. It's a sin, Jhan. Every time I go to the temple, I beg the gentle Ruby Empress to forgive me. I want to stop. I wish I could get away."

Mi had never expressed these feelings to him before, or anything so personal or heartfelt, and yet he wasn't shocked to hear her words. Her manner was nearly always subdued, withdrawn, morose. When she looked up at him again, he saw her bared feelings in her dark eyes. He stepped back into the shed and asked in a low voice, "Do you mean... Would you consider... What if we went away together?"

"Together? Where would we go? If Mommy—"

"I know, but let me think about it, okay?"

"But how could you go away with me, even if I did go? You have to send money home to your parents."

"We both could find other work. Hey, maybe in Haikan! Maybe when I'm there today I can look around a bit, get a sense of things."

"You won't be there long enough for that, and Daddy won't let you go off to look about on your own."

"Let me just think about this a bit, okay? Let me try to work out some possibilities. But would you do that? Go away with me, if it is possible?"

Mi glanced toward the quietly murmuring pressure cooker, her black hair hanging damp upon her shoulders from the heat—the shed itself a kind of pressure cooker—strands of it stuck to her forehead. "Maybe, Jhan."

The truck's horn beeped. Was that for him? Jhan nodded at her and started to turn away, but once again Mi called him back. "Jhan?"

He squinted into the shed again. "Yes?"

"Do you feel the same way? About the cats? When there are cubs, I'm the one who feeds them, like their mother. I *hold* them. They *purr*, Jhan." He couldn't tell from out here in the glare if there were tears in her eyes, and her voice was muffled behind the mask, but he thought so. "Don't you feel as I do about them?"

"I...I don't know," Jhan said. He immediately regretted his honesty though. He should have just said yes. Here was Mi actually entertaining the possibility of running away with him! He should have said yes.

The truck beeped again, and Uncle Zep called out, "Hey! Jhan! Damn you, Jhan, where are you?"

He broke eye contact with Mi and trotted away.

*   *   *

Haikan was so unlike the rural area where Jhan lived with his uncle that going there felt like traveling to another country altogether—or so he imagined. Though nowadays tourists journeyed to the Unnamed Country, its strict government allowed few of its own citizens to go abroad, for fear they wouldn't return. It was a small enough country as it was, tucked in a gap between its neighbors and separated from them by imposing forested mountains. Long ago, the great Emperor Tho had renamed this land what translated as the Unnamed Country so that it would have no name to be known by, and thus no name for would-be colonists and enemies to covet it by. It was said, besides, that he had directed an order of monks to cast a spell of invisibility over this land. However, no spot on the satellite-mapped globe could go undetected and avoid attention these days, and were it not for the influence of other countries, Haikan might well not boast its current glossy towers, its fleets of colorful taxis, its city folk in their smart Western fashions. Though, wherever official flags were flown, they were still elusive flags of transparent silk, and the country still proudly wore its name—or rather, proudly wore no name.

The tiger farmers thought they had found a good parking spot right out in front of the Haikan Center, a looming building that housed five floors of mall space, and above that several floors of luxury apartments, topped off with several floors of office space generally rented by foreign businesses. However, a security guard dressed in green as if he were a policeman came over to the truck yelling at Lhop to move, and for a moment Jhan truly feared that Lhop would reach out his window and pull the guard close to do him harm, but they ended up taking a side street and finding a lot to rent a parking space in. Then, Uncle Zep and Jhan returned to the Haikan Center on foot.

Inside, they inquired as to how to reach those upper levels wherein lay the luxury apartments, since the elevators used by the general public ended at the mall's fifth floor. Uncle Zep gave his cell number, and the guard phoned their client to confirm they were indeed expected. With this matter settled, the uniformed guard escorted them into a hallway off the lobby and to another elevator, opened this by scanning a pass card, and they were then able to ascend. Before the door closed them in, though, the guard looked them up and down with clear distaste. Uncle Zep and Jhan both wore their newest, cleanest t-shirt and cargo shorts, and Jhan's t-shirt even bore the logo for a Western rock band, but apparently the guard still found their appearance questionable, given their destination.

When they emerged from the elevator, it was into a spotless carpeted hallway with one of the doors that lined it already standing open. A woman held the door, and Jhan almost gasped when he saw her. She was young—he guessed about his own age—tallish and slender, wearing a traditional tight-fitting, long-sleeved robe with a high collar and slit sides, made of transparent silk like the nation's flag. Under this she wore a black bra to match her loose-fitting black pants. She was as unrealistically beautiful as a foreign video game character, and by comparison made his pretty cousin Mi seem almost as plain as a useful farm animal.

"Welcome," she said to the tiger farmers as they approached her. "I am Mr. Juong's assistant, Yem. Please, come inside."

Uncle Zep stepped in first, and immediately began removing his sandals. Jhan followed his example, though there were no clusters of flipflops and sneakers in the vicinity of the door as one would expect.

"Oh, that isn't necessary, please," the young woman said. "Mr. Juong is expecting you. May I bring you a beverage?"

Both men declined, and so Yem brought them into another room to introduce them to her master.

The well-fed and well-attired Mr. Juong rose from a chair of more fanciful than accurate Western design, grinning at them. "Ah, my friends, welcome! Please, please, have a seat. Has my assistant offered you a drink? Tea?"

Toward the back of the spacious living room, with its elevated and expansive view of Haikan, two teenaged girls who had been playing with their state-of-the-art cell phones bolted up from a sofa and scurried off into a hallway shyly. Jhan reconsidered that they might not even be teenaged. More doubtful was that they were Mr. Juong's daughters.

Again the men declined beverages, and they sat, and soon—after polite inquiries from Mr. Juong about how their long drive had gone—business was launched into.

Mr. Juong said, "So I'm told that you, Mr. Zep, have the most successful jade tiger farm in all of our country, and that not only can you provide me with bone glue, but bone glue made from cats killed in the wild, as opposed to those raised in captivity. Is this so?"

Uncle Zep clasped his hands before him and leaned forward from the sofa he sat on, recently vacated by those young bottoms. "That is true, sir! I can, most assuredly!"

Mr. Juong smiled, but his eyes were wily, and he absorbed this avowal for a moment before asking, "And how is that so, when I hear there are only a few handfuls of the jade tigers still in the wild?"

"A good question, sir, which I understand you should ask! As it so happens, my family home is quite close by the forest in which these cats were always most plentiful in their heyday. This is why I have any cats to breed at all. I know precisely the areas that are most promising to encounter these animals, rare though they might be. Therefore, I am confident that I can move in and take one of the wild cats when the need arises. Not easily, mind you—such an endeavor could never be easy—but it is, relatively speaking, more easy for me to accomplish than it would be for any other person you might contact."

"Then it seems I have been introduced to just the right people," said Mr. Juong. "You see, I know you could provide me readily enough with bone glue made from farm-raised tigers, and though that would be impressive in itself, we all know that the most potent bone glue comes from those tigers that are brought down, instead, in the wild. Needless to say, I understand their rarity. So, you will, of course, understand my need to see *proof* that the tiger you kill for me has been found in the wild, and not raised on your farm."

"Yes, of course, of course!" Uncle Zep said avidly, grinning, while his nephew Jhan knew that his father's brother lied all the while.

*   *   *

Whenever Jhan's uncle made a trip to Haikan, before returning home he would take the time to visit the great temple of the Jade Emperor, one of the Ten Jeweled Gods and the one with whom Uncle Zep felt the most affinity. Jhan didn't have a favorite god himself, unless you could count the Monkey God, Cholukan, scribe to the gods and the personal pet of the Ruby Empress. Everyone loved the TV series and video game inspired by the trickster Cholukan's wild adventures. Jhan knew that the compassionate Ruby Empress was the god his cousin Mi felt most devoted to, but this was no surprise, since that beautiful divinity was the favorite of most adherents, female or male.

Jhan believed his uncle felt closest to the Jade Emperor because this stern, very masculine god was said to be a great hunter, who since the start of creation had tracked down and eliminated many demons who had escaped the netherworld and attempted, like the spies or terrorists of Western movies, to infiltrate the heavens, bent on evildoing.

The ten great temples to the gods were dispersed throughout the sprawling city of Haikan, but not in some random way. They had been erected at the intersections of dragon paths, and through these invisible lines of earth force the temples communicated with each other, compounding their energy. Viewed from a satellite's perspective, a curious diagram might be created by tracing the lines between these temples, and this resultant symbol figured prominently within the ornate artworks of the temples themselves.

Lhop accompanied them into the temple, as the Jade Emperor was naturally enough his favorite of the Ten Jeweled Gods as well. The three men left their shoes outside, bought a package of incense, and held the smoking joss sticks to their foreheads as they knelt before the gold-painted statue of the Jade Emperor. Large as that statue was, glowering down at them from his altar, it was nothing compared to the temple itself—which was, like all the ten great temples, fashioned in the shape of that particular divinity. In essence, they knelt within the body of the Jade Emperor himself. When they were done and left the temple, Jhan again tilted his head back to appreciate the gargantuan body looming above him and the city buildings around it, dingy and humble in contrast. With the sun glimmering on his massive, muscled body, the Jade Emperor gazed off broodingly toward one of his distant fellow gods (or, being a god, perhaps meeting eyes with all nine of them at once).

Jhan saw a few swifts come flying out of the god's slightly parted lips, like words he uttered that would be conveyed to one of the other gods; words which no human might comprehend.

Jhan was sure Uncle Zep and Lhop had prayed to the Jade Emperor for success in the mission they had taken on today. He himself, though, had asked the god for something else. He had asked for Mi to return his love and go away with him…though he was sure the Ruby Empress would have been a far more sympathetic listener to such entreaties. In fact, Jhan almost feared that the Jade Emperor, in disgust at his weak-minded groveling for love, might even purposely thwart him simply out of spite.

The men returned to Lhop's truck, parked in the temple's large and crowded lot, and embarked on the long ride home. Jhan watched the grimacing titanic representation of the Jade Emperor recede into the distance, a menacing silhouette with a blazing halo of sunlight, like a monster in a foreign movie determined to stomp a puny human city into rubble.

Sitting up front beside Lhop, Uncle Zep asked, "Didn't you mention once you'd been to the site of one of the temples of the Ten Demon Lords?"

Jhan almost shuddered at the mention of this topic. Just as there were Ten Jeweled Gods in the Ten Realms of Heaven, so were there a corresponding Ten Demon Lords of Hell. Such was the harmony of the universe, that even evil needed to exist so as to strike a balance with goodness—not to mention that the Jeweled Gods permitted Hell to exist as a place where sinners might face eternal damnation and endless torture.

"I did," Lhop replied almost casually, staring straight ahead as he gripped the wheel. One got used to his voice, made odd by his lack of an upper lip behind his bogus mustache. "Some years ago, while hunting black bear in the forest, two companions and I chanced upon one such site. We didn't know what it was at first. It seemed like this huge shallow crater in the forest floor, and we wondered if it might be a dried-up pond, but it was perfectly round, so then we thought it might be where a rock had fallen from the sky. Going down into the depression, we finally realized what it was, and then we couldn't climb out of there fast enough. Before we realized it, though, one of my friends put his ear to the ground where there was a gap, a kind of hole like the mouth of an animal burrow, and he heard water dripping down into an underground pool. That explained why the crater hadn't become a pond itself. But also, he claimed to hear an evil little laugh down there, like when someone can't restrain himself from giggling."

"Dear gods," Uncle Zep said.

"I'm not saying that episode had anything to do with it for sure, but about four years later my same friend—who had become an alcoholic, by the way—propped his hunting rifle under his jaw and blew his head apart."

"Oh, I'm sure it had something to do with that," said Uncle Zep, wagging his head. "Can you imagine him remembering that giggling voice night after night when he tried to sleep? That laughter living in his head? Maybe the demon itself lived in his head after that day!"

This time Jhan *did* shudder.

He had always thought it was only a rumor, because who would have gone to so much trouble as to create ten great temples for the Ten Demon Lords of Hell, corresponding to the temples of the Ten Jeweled Gods? These, too, were said to be positioned in such a way, at very particular distances from each other, as to form another—and unholy—symbol, commonly associated with the underworld (a symbol favored as a tattoo by a notorious gang of criminal youths in Haikan, who spraypainted that sigil to mark their territory, in imitation of Western gangs). Furthermore, these ten temples were said to have been built *below* the surface of the earth, pointing downward toward the underworld rather than rearing majestically into the sky. Inverted, and thus the opposites of the ten great temples to the Jeweled Gods…empty of monks, of course, and devoid of visiting worshippers. Existing solely to maintain some sort of cosmic balance.

Who would really go through all the work of constructing such temples, only to have them remain buried and their sites willfully kept secret from common folk? Well, supposedly Emperor Tho himself, the greatest of the Unnamed Country's mortal rulers, had ordered their construction—for who else but Emperor Tho could have devised and orchestrated so ambitious a project?—but Jhan had always taken that for just another part of the myth.

Jhan told himself that Lhop and his old friends had been mistaken about that circular hollow they'd found in the jungle. It had to be where a meteor had fallen, as Lhop himself had suggested, or the site of a pond before the water had drained away, as in a sink, into a cavern beneath.

And the giggling demonic voice? An echo of dripping water misinterpreted. A phantom of the imagination, from the same place where nightmares were made. For even bear hunters could become like children when nightmares came hunting for *them*.

*   *   *

Jhan barely had fifteen minutes to himself during his entire stay in Haikan, but at one point prior to their temple visit, while Uncle Zep and Lhop smoked in a café, he slipped away ostensibly to use a restroom and managed to buy several Western candy bars, which he passed to Mi upon his return home to their mold-stained house of cement-coated brick at the edge of the jungle.

She was in the process of bottling some of the bone glue into their little brown vials when he found her. She wore her mask against the shed's stench of death, but he heard a smile in her voice when she thanked him.

"You were right," he said quietly. "I had no time at all to look into work, but in a city like that there are all sorts of jobs…countless jobs. Have you given any more thought to us going there?"

"Please, Jhan, not now. It's too much to think about right now."

"But you will? Think about it?"

She hesitated, then whispered, "Yes."

He watched her strong, calloused hands seal off the vial she had filled. Jade tiger bone glue was valued for the treatment of rheumatism, but most importantly—as with many of the rare materials hunters and poachers supplied to individual clients and to apothecaries—was valued for its use in stimulating human virility. A man's heightened potency was, one in Jhan's field might well believe, the paramount issue of his species.

Recently, almost as an act of defiance—but also out of curiosity about this elixir with its near-magical reputation, given that he played a part in its production—he had stolen just the slightest bit of bone glue by dipping the handle of a spoon into one of the vials and then swirling that in a little bit of rice wine he had hidden away. He had then drunk all this down and lay in the tiny bedroom his uncle had afforded him, staring up at his ceiling, as if waiting for some miraculous surge of manly hunger. And he did become hungry, though he later wondered if that had only been because, at his youthful, virile age, even having the family's pet cat coil upon his lap might trigger in him a dismaying, undesired arousal. In any case, he'd then had to relieve himself of his built-up hunger, fantasizing about unwary, ruddy-cheeked Mi all the while. After climaxing hard and miserably, he had fallen asleep and dreamed of monkeys growling fiercely in imitation of giant green cats.

-Part 2-

Before the sun had even risen, Aunt Choit wrapped a piece of meat around a segment of kai-mo, the "dream vine," and stuck this on the end of her spear. She then slid the heavy metal spear in through the bars of the cell containing the young tiger that Uncle Zep, Lhop, and Jhan would be taking into the forest this morning. Unlike the sick, aging tiger—which Lhop had been told to dispatch once they'd returned from their trip, and dismantle for parts—this animal, after only a moment of wary hesitation, lunged forward and snatched the offering from the spear tip. The tiger got down on its belly and dug in.

Aunt Choit snorted and said to Jhan, "Soon he'll be grinning at the ceiling like your stupid uncle after he's been drinking rice wine in town."

Kai-mo was a thick, woody vine with the twisted appearance of rope that was only to be found in the deepest forests of the Unnamed Country. Jhan had heard that two Western tourists had been deported once for trying to take some kai-mo from the jungle to smuggle back to their own country. Those two had been lucky; a citizen might very well have ended up in front of a firing squad for that offense. Possessing some of the dream vine was even riskier than dealing in bone glue (though it wasn't as valuable), but the bribes Uncle Zep paid to the local police had up to now buffered his tiger farm from investigations by less flexible authorities, whose price of appeasement might prove crippling.

When he'd begun helping care for their animals, Aunt Choit had explained to Jhan that tigers had been seen in the wild nibbling at these vines on their own, then lying blissfully to gaze up into the shifting lattice of forest leaves, dazzled by sparks of sunlight.

"Your uncle isn't the only animal that likes to get drunk," she'd told him at that time. "Some monkeys like to dig up a special root called goc-jiac. That stuff only grows in our country too. If these things were legal, our country would be a leading force in exports! Animals will eat mushrooms, lichen, all kinds of natural plants to drug themselves. Even bees do it! They like to drink fermented nectar. Apparently it isn't just humans that like to escape from the harsh realities of life." She'd barked a laugh at her own words. "Do you think I should have been a teacher or a philosopher, Jhan?"

"A teacher of philosophy, Auntie."

Now, as she leaned her spear against the wall, she said, "When he's soaked that up for a while, it'll be safe to move him to the truck. He might still be out of it by the time you've taken your pictures and put him back in the truck again."

"I'll let Uncle Zep know when he looks ready," Jhan promised.

"I gave him a good strong dose, because you're going to have to go far enough into the forest to convince that customer of ours this beast was killed in the wild, not raised here from a cub. Your uncle needs to photograph him in a place with features the customer will recognize as deep forest—like trees with kai-mo vines, for instance."

"Yes, he told me that."

Aunt Choit looked closely into his face and smiled strangely. "Did your uncle ever tell you the story of the Western parachutists?"

"Western...men with parachutes? Were those the two who went into the jungle to find kai-mo?"

"No, no... This was many years ago, when our neighbor was at war with their country. Some people say these three Western soldiers were deserters who crossed the mountains on foot and came down into our forest, but I find that hard to believe. Those mountains are not easily crossed, even by people familiar with the region. Instead, I believe the story that says the men meant to parachute into enemy territory, or their plane was shot down, but an updraft from the mountains carried them off...and it was our forest they came down into instead."

Jhan felt that this story was far less plausible than the idea that the men had been deserters who had crossed the mountainous border of the Unnamed Country, but he didn't want to disagree with her, nor interrupt her story, so he just kept listening.

"The three Westerners descended, but the parachute of one of them became tangled in a tree. Before his fellows could cut him down, a jade tiger of unusual size sprang from the brush and they had to abandon their friend…but they heard his bloodcurdling screams. Later when they returned, now with their pistols ready, they found their friend hanging there dead, still in his harness but with both his legs torn off at the knee."

"Dear gods," Jhan hissed.

"The remaining two were forced to go on without him, to seek shelter and try to radio for help, or whatever else they might do to survive. Now, you may ask yourself… *Did* they survive? Were they rescued? Or did they eventually fall prey to tigers or some other horrid fate themselves? No one knows."

"Then…then how do we know this much of the story, Auntie?"

"Through conjecture. You see, years later hunters discovered a moldering parachute snagged in a tree, and two others on the ground nearby, but no one has ever found the remains of any of the three parachutists themselves. *However*…hunters have also reported catching glimpses of a pair of white-skinned men with long gray hair and beards, sneaking through the forest like animals, wearing only loincloths made from camouflaged material."

"Oh my!"

"The question is simply: Are they savages, gone mad from the ordeals of war…or are they now *ghosts* of those soldiers-turned-savages?"

"I don't know which would be more frightening!"

"I tend to think it's ghosts at this point, because it's also said that one can sometimes hear the ghastly screams of that soldier dangling from the trees as a tiger shreds his legs to the bone. Eh, but who knows… Perhaps that's only monkeys screaming, or some other animal." Aunt Choit smiled strangely again.

"That's horrifying!"

"Well, ask Lhop about all this sometime; he's the one who told me. He never saw the white-skinned pair himself, but he knows of a hunter who did."

"I will… I'll ask him sometime."

"Anyway, enjoy your visit to the forest today." Aunt Choit gave his ribs a jab with her elbow, then left the basement to see to packing some supplies for the men's trip.

When she had gone, Jhan's awe changed to disbelief, then to bitterness, and he muttered, "I think she made that up on the spot just to frighten me. Parachutists blown over the mountains, then turned to savages who turned to ghosts. Bah!"

Jhan looked in at the tiger, and found it staring steadily out at him, as if studying his reaction to Aunt Choit's tall tale, its drugged meat totally consumed. So far he detected nothing unusual in the creature's demeanor. How long would it be before the psychedelic properties took effect?

He glanced over at the leaning spear, its tip still greasy from the meat. The tip had plunged right into the core of kai-mo itself, no doubt. If he ran his tongue along the spear tip, would he be able to sample a hint of the dream vine's natural magic? Of course, he was too afraid to actually try it, especially before embarking on such an important job...it was merely a fanciful thought, forgotten as readily as it had occurred to him.

"Hey!" he said to the tiger. "Go to sleep, will you? The sooner you're in your trance, the sooner we can get on with this mad mission."

The big cat only continued gazing back at him, unblinking.

*   *   *

Jhan took his breakfast—a bowl of noodle soup with tripe and tendon, and a cup of instant three-in-one coffee—outside the front of the house where there was a kind of concrete picnic table. It was here that Mi found him, and he was a bit surprised to see her make the effort to seek him out. It was almost always the other way around, unless she was simply relaying an order from Aunt Choit. How exasperating, Jhan found it, that the two of them practically had to hide from each other, pretend the other was invisible, while living under the same roof.

Mi looked this way and that, then came closer to Jhan and bent down a little. Though it was wonderful to see her entire face without her cloth mask, he had to resist gazing down the front of her top where it hung open, providing a glimpse of her delicate breasts almost to their nipples. Her long hair brushed his forearm as she whispered, "Jhan, is it true that you three aren't going to kill Khup today?"

Jhan's brain seized up for a moment, overwhelmed by Mi's nearness and his confusion as to what she was asking him. "Khup?" he managed to repeat.

"The young tiger you helped Mommy feed some dream vine."

Khup? So, Mi had given that cat a name and hadn't shared it with him? Hadn't shared it with anyone? Surely, she was the only one in the house who named the jade tigers; did she have a name for each of them? Even the dead ones, whose bones she fed to the pressure cooker?

"Oh...no, no, we aren't going to kill him." Jhan went on to explain the mission into the forest, sketching in some background about the rich client they had visited in Haikan.

"Oh, that's good, that's good," she said, in plain relief.

"It is," Jhan agreed, this time determined to show Mi that he, too, was sympathetic to the situation of the animals they either raised here, or trapped and brought here themselves, or purchased from other trappers.

Mi glanced about nervously again, then lay her small hand, moist with sweat, on Jhan's forearm where her hair had teased across his flesh. "I'll go with you, Jhan," she said. "We'll find a way, just like you said, okay? When you come back, we can talk about it more."

"Yes!" Jhan said, almost too loudly, unable to prevent a grin from splitting his youthful but sun-leathered face. "Yes, Mi, yes! When I come back, we'll work it all out!"

"I have to go," she said. She even squeezed his arm before releasing it, standing upright, and backing away from the table. Then, she turned and darted off so swiftly, like a frightened deer, that it left Jhan almost fearing he had imagined the whole thing, as if someone had drugged his coffee when he wasn't looking.

*　　*　　*

Jhan had the dream while Lhop's old truck bounced and rattled along the ever narrower, ever rougher dirt road that would take them as far as any path penetrated into the outer reaches of the forest.

In his dream, the truck had already reached the end of the trail, now only barely discerned ruts depressed into the grass and underbrush. He stood back watching Uncle Zep unlock the double doors at the rear of the little truck's box, where the tiger—Khup, he now thought of it—had been hidden during the drive, jostled in its drugged dreams, while Lhop brought closer the homemade sled they would use to drag the cat even deeper into the forest on foot. This was the first time, as far as Jhan knew, that they had used this sled to convey a tiger *into* the jungle, instead of bringing a captured or killed tiger *from* the jungle. Perhaps this new scheme of theirs would become a regular practice henceforth?

While he stood watching his uncle, Jhan's cell phone vibrated in his pocket. He was surprised by this, as he had thought that there was no cell phone reception out this far. He pulled the phone from the pocket of his shorts and was disappointed to see it wasn't Mi trying to reach him with some ideas for their escape plan. Rather, it was his Aunt Choit, and he took the call.

"Hello, Auntie?"

"Jhan!" his aunt practically screamed into his ear. "Mi was just cleaning the cage of the tiger you have with you, and she found something pushed under the straw…"

While he listened to his aunt, he also heard the rear doors of the truck begin to squeal open.

She went on, "It was the piece of dream vine I tucked inside the meat! The cat ate the meat all around it, then hid the kai-mo under the straw! It did it on purpose, I'm sure! It isn't really drugged, Jhan... *It isn't really drugged!*"

In horror, Jhan spun toward the open back of the truck, a depthless black maw, surely deeper than the box was long, and a roar came from within it like a rumbling train that was about to emerge from a tunnel...

Jhan awoke in the back seat of the truck with a gasp so harsh he would have thought the two men up front would have heard it, but apparently they hadn't, busy as they were chatting with each other.

Jhan twisted around in his seat to look behind him, but of course the cab's rear window only gave him a view of the blank metal surface of the box. In the box's darkness, was Khup just then looking up at the same sheet of metal, but from the other side?

"Just a dream," Jhan grumbled to himself. "Stupid Aunt Choit—you did this to me."

Uncle Zep, perhaps having heard him awake with a gasp after all, said without looking around, "Almost at the end of the road, Jhan."

*   *   *

All three of them had wrapped the mossy-furred tiger in the tarp it lay upon in the back of the truck, then awkwardly lowered it outside and transferred it to the sled contraption. Its paws had been bound together, front paw to front paw and rear paw to rear paw, but its head was without a muzzle, the animal's fanged mouth gaping as it exhaled its furnace-like breath. Its eyes stared open, perhaps awake, but not in any ordinary sense. At one point while they handled the beast, Uncle Zep's left hand was close to its mouth, and Jhan said, "Careful, Uncle!" He was remembering his dream.

Uncle Zep only scoffed. "Don't worry... Right now this fool is thinking he's still a cub floating in his mother's womb."

Lhop slung his military carbine over his shoulder, and Jhan wore a student's bookbag for a backpack, containing their lunches and some other supplies. Thus prepared, they began pushing into the rainforest, a seemingly infinite realm of green-upon-green, leaving the locked truck behind. Uncle Zep and Lhop pulled the ropes of the sled to which they had strapped the drugged tiger, with the understanding that after a little while Jhan would take his turn pulling, the three planning to switch one person out every fifteen minutes so that none of them overexerted himself. Still, in rough patches Jhan had the unenviable position of bending down and grabbing the rear edge of the sled, trying to lift it somewhat or at least guide it.

Up front, Lhop used the machete he had brought to hack a clearer path for them. They switched off using this as well, though wielding it at the tough vegetation would prove almost more exhausting for Jhan than pulling at the sled.

After an hour of rotating in these duties, they came to a tree that Lhop specifically had in mind, familiar with it from his bear-hunting days. It was a massive thing with wide, flaring buttress roots; a deciduous tree, though at this time of year it had not shed its leaves. Lhop claimed it was four hundred years old, and from the look of the monster, Jhan could believe it.

"This will do nicely," Uncle Zep huffed, throwing down the loop of rope he'd slung over his shoulder, then massaging the spot where it had dug in.

"We aren't looking for some dream vine to pose it beside?" Jhan asked.

"We don't have to get that particular. Anyone could see from this spot that we're deep in the forest."

The trio took the edges of the tarp and hefted the animal onto the ground, grunting as they supported about a hundred pounds each. Straightening, Uncle Zep kneaded the small of his back now instead of his shoulder, while Lhop used his knife to cut away the bonds around the cat's front and back limbs. Then, the three of them worked together once more to roll the tiger off the tarp and onto the forest floor in a spot sheltered between two of the great tree's sweeping buttress roots.

Jhan dragged the tarp away so it wouldn't show in the photographs they were going to take. Likewise, Lhop dragged the sled off to one side.

Returning, Lhop pointed to a scattering of initials carved into the tree's smooth, silvery bark. Jhan hadn't noticed any of these markings before. None looked fresh, but some appeared quite old, almost swallowed by the tree's hard flesh and so distorted they were now impossible to decipher.

"We want to get these carvings in some of the shots," he said. "That way, if our customer doubts us, this specific tree proves that we came this far into the forest."

"Good idea, Uncle Lhop," Jhan said. Lhop wasn't his uncle, but addressing him thusly was a common sign of respect for a young person like himself.

"Learn from our craftiness, Jhan," Uncle Zep said, grinning, as he took a sip from a can of refreshing white fungus drink he had taken from his nephew's backpack. He tapped Jhan's temple with one learned finger.

"Do you have a loved one whose initials you want to carve in the tree with your own?" Lhop teased.

Jhan wondered if this was some kind of test pertaining to Mi. Or did Lhop really wonder if there might be some girl Jhan saw in town on his infrequent visits there alone? He tried not to blush as he replied, "Not yet, Uncle Lhop."

"Have you carved your initials there, Lhop?" Uncle Zep chuckled.

"No, though I wouldn't mind carving my initials into the heart of a couple women I've known."

Jhan smiled uneasily.

"Just think," Uncle Zep said. "With this new tactic of ours, we can claim this one tiger's death out here over and over again. Why, I wish I'd thought to have us all bring a few changes of clothes, so we could take a series of photos in advance, just repositioning ourselves a bit each time." He laughed heartily at this concept. "We could save ourselves a number of return journeys."

Emboldened by his uncle's good spirits, and because today he almost felt like a partner to these men and not just a somewhat useful child, Jhan said, "They say there are only maybe thirty jade tigers left out here, Uncle. What do we do when they're gone, and we have no cubs on the way, only the last cats in our cages?"

"They say, they say," Uncle Zep mocked. "Who is 'they'? Foreign busybodies who don't have to scrape for a living? Who try to scare us and bully us, because they care more about beasts than human beings? Lhop says there may be well over a hundred, maybe a hundred-fifty tigers left in the forests and mountains, eh, Lhop?"

"More than thirty, anyway," Lhop said conservatively.

"We like our clients to think there are that few, so they value the services we provide. Anyway, even if they did die out, and we couldn't mate any that we have at the farm, then we'd...we'd go into the black bear business, I suppose. Make bear bone glue, and bear bile drink and whatnot. A lot less valuable, but less risky to deal in because bears aren't protected. So it would be bears...eh, Lhop?"

Lhop, with his plastic nose, didn't respond.

Uncle Zep walked over to Jhan and dug around in his backpack again, but this time what he extracted was an old plastic water bottle that he had filled with ox blood. He handed this to Jhan.

"Here, you pour it. My back is killing me."

"Will you tell me where?" Jhan asked. He didn't want to mess up this enterprise with any missteps.

"Yes, yes. We're going to do some on the chest, to simulate a wound to the heart, then some in the mouth to simulate vomited blood. You see this?" Uncle Zep dug a condom packet out of a pocket of his shorts. He tore open this sleeve, withdrew the rolled condom. "We're going to place this onto the chest first, then pour enough blood over it that it will look like there's at least some kind of circular wound there. You see what I mean? Craftiness. You have to be inventive!"

Lhop said, "Now that I think of it, I have some chewing gum in the truck. I should have brought it with me. I could have chewed up a few pieces, then shaped a bullet wound out of that."

"Oh!" said Uncle Zep. "What a great idea! Oh, Lhop, why didn't you bring that with you? It's too far to go back just for that."

"I could go alone. Without the sled, it wouldn't take nearly as long."

"No, no... I want to get this over with. Anyway, the beast won't sleep forever. We'll go with my idea."

Ultimately, Uncle Zep wasn't happy with how the condom looked on the tiger's chest, with the ox blood poured over it and running down the animal's side like new stripes at odds with its natural stripes. Lhop suggested they soak some of the paper napkins Aunt Choit had packed with their lunches, and shape a mock wound from those. Lhop took over the operation, and Uncle Zep was pleased with this result.

"You are a true artist, Lhop! Jhan, now pour some into its mouth."

"Yes, Uncle." Jhan stepped closer to Khup's open-eyed, open-mouthed head and crouched down. He saw one of the cat's ears twitch instinctively at his nearness.

Meanwhile, Uncle Zep turned to Lhop. "Hand me your rifle, will you? Of course, it makes sense to have me act the hunter in this shot, not you, since our client didn't meet you. I made sure to wear the same t-shirt I did that day, and he'll know my body type. Then again, we don't want these photos to end up in the wrong hands, so..." Having said this, while Lhop unslung his carbine from his back, over his lower face Uncle Zep hooked a cloth mask, like those that motorbike riders used to keep from inhaling dust and vehicle exhaust. He then donned a pair of dark glasses and accepted the rifle Lhop held out to him.

"Ah yes, I feel like the great hunter!" Uncle Zep, who was no great hunter, joked. He glanced over to watch as Jhan carefully began trickling some of the ox blood into the drugged tiger's mouth. "Hey," he said, "don't just pour that down its throat now... We need to see it in the photos. Pour some around the *outside* of its mouth."

Jhan shifted the dribble of ox blood from Khup's maw to its muzzle, where the greenish fur gave way to white, and as he did so the cat's huge pink tongue—covered in barbs like countless tiny fangs—curled up to lick the blood away.

Jhan jolted.

Two things happened at precisely the same time then, as if the two animals had been in telepathic communication with each other, which of course was impossible—as far as Jhan knew.

Jhan had looked around to tell his uncle, with some alarm, that he thought the cat was starting to come out of its stupor. As he turned away, the tiger's tongue extended again, toward the bottle he held, and its surface rasped across the back of his hand. When a tiger licked in a casual way, it might feel only like sandpaper, but when greater pressure was exerted it could strip feathers, fur, even flesh from its prey. The resulting abrasion was just enough to raise tiny beads of blood on Jhan's skin.

When he looked up to address his uncle at the same instant the tiger dragged its powerful tongue across his skin, Jhan saw an older jade tiger—perhaps a hundred pounds heavier than Khup—come crashing out of the brush at Lhop. Lhop was already in the process of spinning toward it when it came, maybe having heard its approach at the last second, and he hadn't even completed the move before he started throwing himself off to one side in a desperate dive.

"Hey!" Uncle Zep cried out, whirling toward the animal too. He was still holding the rifle, and he brought it up to his shoulder quickly, but fumbled with the safety.

Jhan jerked his hand away from Khup and returned his attention to the drugged cat in horror, throwing himself backward so abruptly that he fell onto his rump. He dropped the water bottle, and ox blood gushed to the ground.

Lhop executed something like a roll, came back up on his feet, and bolted frantically toward the forest at a right angle to the big tiger's path of attack. The cat corrected for this easily though, and was beginning to leap after the man when Uncle Zep began firing. In his terror, and being no experienced marksman, Jhan's uncle emptied the entire fifteen-shot magazine as fast as he could pull the trigger, pointing at the moving target rather than aiming.

Jhan scrambled to his feet, and just before he plunged into the jungle himself, he saw one of the wildly spraying bullets smash through the outer orbit of the tiger's right eye in a burst of misting blood. Somehow, instead of killing the cat, all this did was get it to change its choice of prey. When Jhan lost sight of his uncle, the tiger had wheeled around and came charging at him instead, with Lhop apparently having successfully vanished into the forest's depthless green-upon-green.

As Jhan dashed madly through the jungle, gulping at the humid air and unmindful of the machete-like leaves that slashed at his face and arms, he heard Uncle Zep's high-pitched screams receding behind him.

-Part 3-

Jhan crouched behind another of those enormous trees like the one where they had meant to pose with Khup, catching his breath as he tried to use his cell phone. He hadn't really expected to get reception, had he? He couldn't call for help, couldn't access the map feature to determine just exactly where he was. He had thought he was striking out in the direction from which they had come with the sled, hoping to get back to the truck, but nothing he saw around him had looked familiar. It was a sameness of overly lush vegetation, crowding out even the sky. Anyway, even if he did find his way back to the truck, Lhop had locked it up in case other poachers chanced upon it. He hoped Lhop got to it first, unlocked it, and used its horn to guide him.

Lhop was fast, strong, experienced. As for Uncle Zep, Jhan entertained no hope.

Tucking his phone back into his shorts, still squatting behind the tree with sweat streaming down his lower back, Jhan checked the back of his right hand. Though the beads had already dried to so many tiny dark scabs, the area where Khup had licked him burned, was even reddened. Was that simply irritation from the abrasion, or could the area already be infected?

He was too nervous to eat anything from the lunches still in his backpack, but he was parched from running and fished out a can of white fungus drink, drained it in a few gulps, and returned the empty can to his bag. He looked around inside for anything to use as a weapon, but even if he'd found a knife—which he didn't—what were the odds of him using it effectively if the one-eyed tiger caught up with him? He did, however, find a half-empty box of shells for the rifle, but that was back with his uncle's body.

His bladder had been harassing him for a while, but he had been reluctant to empty it for fear that the scent of his urine would attract the enraged tiger to him. However, he couldn't hold it any longer, so he stood, unzipped, and pissed onto the trunk of the sheltering tree.

As he did this, his gaze lifted to where some markings had been carved into the bark. At first, horrified, he thought he had accidentally circled back to the tree where the three of them had been attacked, but he remembered that tree was even larger than this one, and this carving was not the initials of lovers.

Though the tree's growth had caused these lines to become less distinct over time, to the point where parts of the carving had been erased, Jhan could make out enough to determine it meant to represent the head of a demon, with flared bull-like horns and a third eye in its forehead.

"Gods protect me," Jhan murmured, backing away from the mysterious visage.

He continued along, still hoping—with decreasing faith—that he was headed toward the truck. As he went, he scanned the ground for a fallen branch that might be long and straight enough to use as a spear. He no longer ran, for fear that his reckless sounds would draw attention to him. Instead, he stole along like a hunter instead of the hunted.

*   *   *

He might not be able to make a call on his phone, nor use its GPS feature, but it still told the time...and he saw that it had been over two hours since the tiger attack. For some of that time he'd been running, and he hadn't been pulling a heavy sled at all. And yet, from the truck to the four-hundred-year-old tree it had only taken about an hour.

Unless he was not heading in a straight line, and might eventually curve that way accidentally, it was clear he was not moving in the direction of Lhop's little truck.

As far as Jhan knew, he had gone the *opposite* way...deeper into the heart of the jungle. There would be no villages secreted in its depths, with people who could lend him aid. If his suspicion was correct, and he kept going that way, the jungle floor would finally begin to angle upward, transitioning into steep foothills, then to rugged mountains, so that—owing to the cooler elevations—the type of trees themselves would show a change, ultimately becoming mostly pines. Oh, there were villages high in the mountains, such as the one where he'd been living with his parents before moving in with Uncle Zep, but those were reached only by a few roads that circumnavigated the thickest region of the rainforest, where they had ventured.

Why did he keep moving then, he asked himself, if it was only to worsen his situation? For one thing, he still hoped that Lhop—who had escaped deeper into the jungle himself—would reconnect with him, but mostly he supposed he was simply afraid that if he didn't keep moving, the one-eyed tiger would catch up to him. He was convinced the creature would still be stalking him, to avenge itself for the injury Uncle Zep had done it. In vengeance, even, for all those jade tigers caged back at home. All of this might be punishment, he thought, meted out by Mi's favorite goddess, the Ruby Empress, sympathetic friend to animals.

Whether it was wise to keep moving or not, as he did so he was finally eating something from his backpack. He'd been reluctant to do so before now, thinking that he might need to make this food last, but also for fear that a tiger or bear might smell the sandwich Aunt Choit had made from cold cuts and pickled vegetables...though, might those animals just as easily smell his sweaty human flesh anyway?

Once, he froze with an audible gasp when to his right he caught a peripheral glimpse of a shaggy black bear lurking in the brush, just waiting to surge out at him, only to look at it directly and see it was in truth the moldering trunk of a fallen tree. And, of course, he glimpsed jade tigers again and again, dozens of them, more than Uncle Zep's wildest estimations, but each time it turned out to be some stirring patch of green vegetation, striped with the shadows of fronds.

With a bite of sandwich in his mouth he again halted in his tracks, having heard a familiar sound just off to his left. It was a sound he had heard Khup make before, and he realized then that after the past several hours the young adult tiger might be mostly recovered from the effects of the dream vine. Then, Jhan recognized the sound for what it was: a series of little cries made by a langur, calling to others of its kind. He remembered this was a sound Khup had cleverly learned to make in imitation of those monkeys, when he'd still lived in the wild as a cub.

Relieved, he resumed walking...like a shark, compelled to continue moving forward lest it stop and die from lack of oxygen passing through its gills.

He tried to remain hyperaware, intensely alert, but he couldn't help remembering a joke he had once heard Lhop, in his strange voice, recite to Uncle Zep, Aunt Choit, Mi, and himself at dinner. The joke revolved around two characters Lhop had told other jokes about: the dimwitted brothers Fuong and Wuong.

"One day, Fuong and Wuong went hunting for wild pigs in the woods, but they ventured in too deep and realized they'd become lost. Fuong grew nervous, and he said, 'Wuong, what will we do?'

"Wuong hoped to keep his younger brother calm, and he said, 'Don't worry… Shoot into the air, and I'm sure help will come.'

"So Fuong shot once into the air, and the two waited a half hour, and yet no help came. Again, Fuong cried, 'Wuong, no one's come for us! What should we do?'

"Wuong kept a brave face and replied, 'Be patient, Fuong. Shoot into the air again… I'm sure this time someone will come.'

"So Fuong shot once more into the air, and again the brothers waited for help to arrive, but after another half hour still no one had come. By now, Fuong was close to panic, and he whined, 'Wuong, this isn't working… What can we do?'

"Wuong stubbornly tried to remain strong, and he said, 'Fuong, you mustn't give up hope. Try it again… Shoot into the air, and someone might discover us yet.'

"To which Fuong replied, 'But, Wuong, I can't shoot anymore—I'm all out of arrows!'"

*　　*　　*

As Jhan pushed the last fragment of sandwich into his mouth, he took note of how red and swollen his right hand had become, his glossy skin hot to the touch. It had to be an infection, and yet so soon? Was it the ox blood that he had poured into the tiger's mouth, having gotten into his system through the abrasion? Or bacteria that naturally lived in the carnivore's mouth?

In fact, now that he stopped to pay attention to how he was feeling, he realized that he wasn't just overheated from exertion and the rainforest's oppressive humidity; he actually felt feverish. He was experiencing the sensation of a head full of fizzing static, like a TV with no reception, that one got when the body was recognizing and responding to some new invading illness.

Standing in one place, he turned in little increments, gazing all around him. Was it his imagination, or did colors seem to bleed beyond their physical confines as he moved, as if the green of this bush or that tree was teased out from its source for a bit before the phenomenon ended, only to be repeated with another plant, and another, as he continued rotating? Extruded trails of glowing green, tapering, then fading…like afterimages…or the glimpsed spirits of primitive living things, normally concealed from the human eye…

Jhan tilted back his head, masticating his sandwich mindlessly, and stared up at the jungle canopy. The afternoon sun dazzled where it flared in the myriad gaps between leaves in mesmerizing shifting patterns, like the gold of sunset scattered upon the surface of a lake. He thought of the burnished scales of the Gold-Scaled Dragon, whose adventures with the Monkey God Cholukan he had enjoyed watching in a popular TV series. He swallowed the bite of sandwich and smiled dreamily, weaving a little where he stood. Gazing upward…remembering the Gold-Scaled Dragon in that series…starting out as Cholukan's nemesis, then later becoming his comrade…

Some little part of his mind, standing back and observing the rest of himself in horror, called out to him nervously. Called for him to awaken, like a mother rousing her child from a feverish dream. The rest of him took notice, and Jhan shook himself out of his reverie. He looked around wildly, afraid that while he had been daydreaming some monster might have been creeping up on him. Fortunately, he saw nothing, but the quick movements of his head only worsened that effect of extruded trails of living green light.

"The kai-mo!" he said aloud, in realization.

Somehow, Jhan was certain, a trace of the dream vine Khup had chewed up with his meat had lingered in his mouth. Somehow, when the beast had licked him with such abrading pressure, it had poisoned his own blood with that psychedelic drug.

"Oh no," he mumbled, instantly feeling all the drunker for knowing he might be drunk, as if his own mind supplied half the effect psychosomatically. "Oh no…"

Not much could have entered into his system, he reasoned—right? The effect couldn't possibly last long. But then again, it had infiltrated his very blood. What he was experiencing had to be the dream vine…had to be. It couldn't merely be the fever of infection…couldn't only be attributed to his state of stress and anxiety…

"Don't panic, Fuong," he said to himself in a shaky little joke. "Someone will come for us."

* * *

Jhan knew the terrain would gradually incline upward if he were ever to reach the foothills of the forested mountains that rose as a wall between the Unnamed Country and its neighbor—though even in his weird delirious state, he was aware he couldn't be anywhere near that far into the jungle yet. What he hadn't expected, however, was for the terrain to angle *downward* so radically and suddenly that he almost toppled over a kind of lip. He recoiled from the edge, thinking that this must be a ravine, deceptively overgrown with vegetation to mask its broken surface. Maybe even with a stream at the bottom.

If it was a stream, good! He had heard that when lost in the woods, it was best to follow a river or stream to prevent wandering in circles. Not to mention, he only had a few more cans of white fungus drink left. He had wisely kept the empty cans to fill with water if he encountered it. Better to drink dirty water than die of thirst...though, it would be better still if he ran across some traveler's palms, since rainwater would run down their great fanned leaves to collect at their bases. As for food, he'd already spotted mangoes in the foliage above him several times, and though he hadn't bothered to get at them, he knew they weren't the only sources of food he might encounter. Finding food wasn't really his concern...his concern was *becoming* food.

Now that he was aware of the abrupt decline, he moved close to its edge again, to look below and see if he was right about a stream. Weaving a little where he stood, as he did whenever he wasn't staggering along with a drunkard's forward momentum, he stared with a dawning understanding of what he was seeing, until he was overcome with terror and wonder...as if he had chanced upon the mossy bones of some expired, gigantic deity.

This had to be the very spot Lhop had described when they'd been driving out here from home...the great shallow bowl in the forest that he claimed to have encountered as a younger man whilst bear hunting with companions. A site that resembled a dried-up pond, yet perfectly round— so perhaps a crater where a meteor might have come down in prehistoric times.

Lhop had said it was the site of one of the alleged hidden temples built for each of the Ten Demon Lords of Hell, to achieve a cosmic equilibrium with the temples for the Ten Jeweled Gods.

He groaned out loud at the unpleasant experience of gazing into the great bowl too long. Admittedly, all the plant life that filled it might be stirring in a hot breeze, but mostly he attributed the movement he was seeing to his altered perceptions...because it was all moving too wildly, as if he watched a storm-tossed ocean, all luminous green. He had to wrench his eyes from the mesmerizing phenomenon and try to take in other details of the scene.

Directly opposite him, also standing at the edge of the hollow but on its far side, was a tree of the same type and size as the four-hundred-year-old specimen where they had planned on posing for photographs with Khup. The tree was so massive that its thick, silvery-gray roots actually spilled over the edge and down into the crater, looking like streams of wax from a melted candle that had solidified. The behemoth's leaves churned unnaturally, like the foliage in the bowl—seething, writhing—but Jhan tried to ignore that effect.

Because the seemingly agitated plant life wasn't giving off any rustling noises as one would expect had the vegetation truly been moving in that way, Jhan was able to hear a strange cry or utterance from the direction of the tree. Some kind of wet snorting sound. Returning, now, as a raspy, phlegmy groan. A tiger messily digging into its meal?

He finally noticed something. Just poking out from behind one of the tree's buttress roots, a little of the sled they had brought for dragging Khup could be discerned.

Jhan's heart leapt in excitement, but his body was still fearfully poised for flight. The presence of the sled didn't mean that there wasn't an animal lurking behind that tree too. He listened for another of those vocalizations, and this time it sounded human to him...just barely. A kind of miserable sob, strangely impeded.

"Lhop?" Jhan cried out. He was taking a risk, but he figured approaching the tree to discover the source of the sound was even riskier.

In response: another inarticulate cry, but a little louder, more urgent if no less distorted.

He had to go investigate. If it had been a tiger making these noises, when he had called out it would have already pounced out from behind the tree and come charging him by now.

Cutting straight across through the crater would be quicker than circling along its edge, but he knew he would have to be careful that he didn't catch his ankle in some broken opening such as Lhop had described, where his comrade had crouched down to listen to water dripping into some mysterious space below and heard eerie, unaccountable giggling besides. A flush of gooseflesh swept over Jhan at the memory of this detail, but be that as it may, he started easing himself down the slanting incline into the hollow itself. No knife or machete in hand, and he had forgotten the idea of fashioning a spear for himself.

The plants growing down in the crater swirled around his legs, stroking his flesh where exposed by his shorts. The vegetation seemed sentient, caressing him with sadistic delight like a cruel lover tormenting a virgin. Having reached the bowl's floor and started across, at one point he tripped a little over a rock or root hidden in the undergrowth, and he looked down sharply, expecting to discover that little opening, but he saw none. Maybe the hole or crack or whatever it had been that Lhop had mentioned had become filled in since he'd chanced upon this place.

Jhan had nearly made it to the other side by now, but he hadn't heard another of those disturbing noises again, after one last gargling sound like someone hocking up a loogie. Then again, the sound of his sneakers crunching through the undergrowth might be drowning out quieter sounds up there.

He was nearing the roots of the tree where they spilled down to the crater's floor and squiggled out from there like blindly searching tentacles. Up close, he could better appreciate how the roots were the thickness and color of elephant trunks. And despite their solidity and obvious great weight, if he looked at them too steadily he could swear he saw the roots shifting, like immense pythons stirring sluggishly.

"No," he whispered to himself. "No, no…"

He was about to tear his gaze from the roots, and bypass the tree to ascend the hollow's far side, when he noticed some carvings on the thickest of them. He slowed his pace, wary, and instead of bypassing the roots he moved in closer to them to be sure of what he was seeing.

Several simple faces, like the one he had discovered hours earlier, on another tree: the visage of a demon, with horns like a bull and a third eye in the forehead. The thing was, all three…no, he saw it was four…oh, and another one, on another of the roots! And another! The thing was, these more or less identical carvings—some a bit more artistically rendered than others—all appeared to have been inscribed in these roots at different times, just like the lovers' initials Lhop had teased him about. Some were so obliterated by time, so filled in as the roots had continued to swell and elongate since they'd been carved that they were almost entirely absorbed. Others were fairly clear, but the inscribed areas had darkened with time. But here was one face where the lines were bright and sharp, as if the demon's face had been carved there only an hour ago.

Jhan muttered under his breath to Mi's favorite god, the Ruby Empress, "Sweet compassionate goddess, please protect me."

He finally resumed moving toward the right, away from the roots, and without much effort climbed up from the great depressed circle. In reaching the jungle floor's regular level again, he turned toward the tree and the sled he had seen poking out just barely from behind it.

The sled had been pulled into a sheltering gap between two of the upswept buttress roots, and a man sat upon it with his back to Jhan, hunched forward a little, his arms apparently resting in his lap. This close to him, Jhan heard a long, spluttering attempt at an intake of breath.

He didn't need to see the man's front to know this was not Lhop, but his Uncle Zep. Even if he hadn't recognized his t-shirt—the same one he had worn when they'd gone to Haikan to see their client—Jhan would recognize him from the back of his head, his haircut. Still, that isn't to say there wasn't something odd about him, even seen from the back.

"Uncle!" Jhan cried, rushing forward to go to him. He saw Uncle Zep flinch, and heard a kind of choked sound, but no words. When he moved around in front of his uncle, he realized why.

The feverish state that had come over Jhan suddenly intensified, his ears hissing with radio static, his vision altering, as if without his permission someone had changed the settings of a TV he was watching, making the colors oversaturated, painful to the eye.

"Gods!" Jhan blurted, falling back a few steps.

Uncle Zep turned one eye up to look at his nephew. One eye was his only remaining identifiable feature. The rest of his face was gone, though admittedly not scooped out—as one might rightly think at first—but torn aside, hanging in a thick flap, inside out. Ragged ends of flesh even hid the teeth of his lower jaw, though his upper jaw appeared to be included in that hanging flap. His skull showed where his forehead had been laid open. Jhan thought his uncle might have been slightly less horrifying to look upon had he not retained that one staring eye. The one-eyed tiger had enacted its revenge all too well.

Woozy, Jhan thought then that it was as if his uncle's face was a theater curtain that had been ripped aside, ripped apart, unveiling to him the secret, raw red meat at the heart of the tangible world. Mortality's wet glistening heart pulsed not only in one organ, but within every cell in every beast mighty and small. Something fragile but eternal.

Jhan felt faint. The formless meat of his uncle's face—or rather, the torn crater where his face had been—appeared to shift and move, and at first he thought this, too, was the effect of the dream vine in his system, until he heard a gurgling sound from his uncle's throat and realized his meat was struggling to draw in air and expel words at the same time, succeeding laboriously only in the first effort.

"Where is Lhop, Uncle?" Jhan asked him. "Lhop dragged you here, didn't he? He had to have! Where is he?"

Just that one staring eye. Though Jhan knew he was not at fault for any of this, had made no missteps that could pin the blame for this tragedy on him, he still felt as though his uncle stared accusingly. That made no sense, no. It was pain only...and not even that, but shock.

Jhan looked around him, and to his surprise saw Lhop's rifle lying on the ground beside the sled. Had he left it for Uncle Zep, and then gone off to find help or return to the truck, carrying just his machete? Jhan went to the gun, picked it up. He had never fired it before, but he had used guns plenty of times in first-person shooter video games at the internet café in town. He found the magazine release, pulled it from the underside of the carbine, and was going to use shells from the box in his backpack to replenish the magazine but saw Lhop had already done so. He fitted the magazine back into place, with a round already in the pipe.

Jhan slung the carbine over his shoulder, then turned back to his uncle, who still eerily kept staring at him, seeming not even to blink, unless his eyelid was ripped away too. It was hard to tell. As he took in his uncle again, a distant part of Jhan's mind wondered if that one eye had been saved partly because Uncle Zep had been wearing his dark glasses, in addition to his cloth face mask, when the big tiger had launched its attack.

"Uncle," Jhan tried again, stooping down a bit as if speaking to a much older person who suffered memory loss. "Where is Lhop?"

Uncle Zep didn't attempt speaking this time, just wheezed and gurgled as he strained to breathe, but one of his hands floated up from his lap, where blood was pooling in the folds of his shorts. His hand, gloved with gore, slowly pointed its finger behind Jhan...toward the circular hollow he had just come up from.

Jhan glanced behind him, then looked back to his uncle. "He went that way? But I came from that way, Uncle...I didn't see him. Are you sure?"

Then Uncle Zep's hand changed direction, dipping down as if his pointing finger were an airplane that had suddenly experienced engine failure, and begun to nosedive.

Jhan's face rumpled in confusion. "Down? Down where?"

Uncle Zep stabbed his finger downward a few times to emphasize his meaning.

Jhan's eye widened. "He went down...underground? Below this crater?"

Uncle Zep returned his hand to his lap. Had he given a little nod? Jhan couldn't tell. He didn't want to look at his face any longer. He couldn't bear the intensity of that single eye's gaze, nor the wounded stirring of the meat parts inside his opened head. He stood straighter, turned away from his uncle, and in so doing found his eyes drawn to the ancient tree.

More of those horned, three-eyed demon faces had been carved into the trunk of the tree itself. How many? Dozens, surely, extending so far up he didn't know how someone could have climbed the wide, smooth trunk that far to render them. Again, they varied greatly in age, from very old to seemingly recent.

As Jhan gawped at the carvings in awe, he saw the third eye in every one of them turn in unison to gaze directly back at him.

He clenched his eyes shut, clenched his teeth, and hissed, "No! No! It's the dream vine!"

Uncle Zep rasped out a loud noise from his blood-clogged throat. His single eye had spotted something, and he meant to warn his nephew…this much Jhan realized when he opened his eyes, looked around, and saw the one-eyed tiger.

*   *   *

Later, in the dark place—when he had more time to ponder it than now—Jhan would wonder about the tiger's thought process (or was it only inscrutable instinct?). Why it again attacked his uncle, instead of him. Was it only because his uncle was just that much closer to the spot in the forest it emerged from? Because his uncle was seated, and more vulnerable, whereas he was on his feet and had some chance of eluding it? Could it not recognize that it was the rifle, and not Uncle Zep himself, that had wounded it, and thus understand it was wiser to take Jhan down before he could use that object of destruction? Or as a mechanical object of destruction itself, did the cat only recognize Uncle Zep as a job it hadn't completed the first time around—presumably driven off by Lhop, who hadn't fled too deeply into the forest after all, but returned in an effort to save his friend's life?

Maybe the creature was just drawn to the blood.

Whatever it thought or didn't think, the one-eyed tiger was on Uncle Zep…knocked him onto his back. Maybe the first time it had gone for the man's throat, but Uncle Zep had instinctively tucked in his chin and it had grasped onto his face instead, but this time when it went for the throat its human prey was too weakened to resist. It clamped on there, its three-inch fangs sunk deep.

Uncle Zep couldn't even squeeze enough air through his throat to make one last wet wheeze before he died.

While this was happening, Jhan was unslinging the carbine from his shoulder, bringing it up to a firing position, trying to trigger it and remembering that the safety was on. It only took a second to resolve this, however, and then—bracing the rifle to his shoulder—he began firing. As he did this, though, he also backed up, to put more distance between himself and the animal lest it abandon its prey to come for him instead.

Jhan had never fired a real rifle, and the recoil jolted him, but he kept pulling the semiautomatic weapon's trigger, shot after shot as Uncle Zep had done when they'd been attacked by this beast the first time. With each shot, he took another quick step backward. He heard a deep rumble of pain from the tiger, and knew he'd hit it somewhere, and it let go of his suffocated uncle and lifted its great head toward him. He looked into its face for a moment…one eye a black pit filled with crusted blood, its white muzzle slathered red with new blood. Its remaining eye—a green gem nested in green fur—locked onto him, and Jhan fired at it.

Again like Uncle Zep, though, he fired out of blind panic rather than with deliberation, and as quickly as his finger could accomplish the action. Ultimately, three things happened all at once. The carbine's fifteen-shot magazine ran empty…and the tiger thumped down heavily on top of his uncle's body, having been struck in the head and elsewhere…and upon the last shot, Jhan went falling backward into empty space.

He had toppled backward over the rim of the crater, but his flight didn't last long. His back thudded painfully into one of the buttress roots that was draped over the side of the depression, and with the air driven out of him, he flopped over the side of that root and onto another just below it. Here, he caught hold of the root and hung on, and he managed not to drop the rifle in the process. The remainder of the fall wouldn't have been far, but he clung there desperately as if poised over a bottomless pit.

Jhan lay belly-down on the massive, slanting root gasping for air, his brain gasping for sanity. He absorbed the reality of the fact that just up there, out of sight, both his uncle and the one-eyed tiger lay dead. He had failed to save his uncle, but he knew that was a mercy. He was too shaken to feel pride at having won in a battle against such a ferocious predator, one of the purest distillations of nature's viciousness.

As he lay there on the root, he realized he was smelling incense.

Was this another trick of the dream vine? Who would be burning incense out here?

He lifted his head a little, sniffing at the air, and inclining his face toward where the scent seemed to be coming from, saw a black gap just beside him, shielded by the tentacle-like roots. Part of a doorway? How long ago might such a passage have been fashioned, if these immense roots had grown over it? Hundreds of years, surely. But…had the open doorway in the side of the crater existed before the roots, or had it purposely been created behind the roots to obscure its existence?

There had to be people within that blackness; incense didn't burn itself. Might it even be Lhop? Lhop wouldn't have left Uncle Zep unattended…not after pulling him this far on the sled, by himself, to elude the tiger that stalked them. But if he wasn't inside that darkness, then where was he? All Jhan knew was that Lhop hadn't been with his uncle any longer.

Someone *had* to be in there…and maybe they could help him find his way back to the truck, or out of the jungle by another path.

He still hoped it was Lhop though... Lhop, having found some incense in there, maybe even burning it so as to guide Jhan. Incense, discovered in what could only be an inverted temple built in recognition of one of the Ten Demon Lords of Hell.

So the legends *were* true? But this begged the question: since there was, apparently, a temple buried beneath this spot, and incense was kept in there, did that mean that there were secret orders of monks whose task it was to inhabit these hidden temples, and enact whatever rites were required to placate or subdue those hateful demon lords?

Would such monks be displeased that he had stumbled upon their temple? Perhaps even dangerously displeased?

Still, he had to seek human assistance. He was done with fighting the monsters of this forest.

And beyond requiring help, there was his curiosity, which had flamed up inside him.

How could he *not* want to know—and witness with his own eyes— what was within that ancient darkness?

-Part 4-

The black opening beside him—from which he was catching that faint waft of incense—was too small for even his slender body to squeeze through, but he looked below him...and behind a root as thick around as a normal tree trunk he saw another, larger area of the mostly concealed doorway. He climbed down to it.

He hesitated at the opening, torn between those strong forces of fear and curiosity. Leaning against the root, he dug out the box of shells from his backpack and again loaded the carbine's magazine with fifteen bullets. That left just five shells in the box.

Then he dug out his cell phone and woke it. He saw its battery only held a charge of 53%. He wished he hadn't been playing games on it during part of their drive out here. It couldn't be helped now. He activated the phone's flashlight feature, held it out in front of him, and passed through the opening between the roots.

There were other smells within this space, stronger than the hint of incense that pierced through them, and they enclosed him immediately just like the darkness. Damp, mold, the ammonia stench of rat or bat feces. The light from Jhan's phone revealed that the walls of this subterranean passage were matted with layers of spiderwebs, though thankfully there were none strung across his path. And his path led downward…down a flight of stairs, which like the walls were manmade, though the stairs appeared to be blocks of dark green marble, whereas the walls were covered in what he guessed were ceramic tiles, also the color of jade. Some of the rows were buckled, with occasional tiles missing, groping roots having pushed through the hard-packed dirt where the tiles had been set.

The staircase curved down toward what would be the area directly below the hollow in the jungle floor. Jhan descended the steps slowly, carefully, because marble could be slippery and there were no handrails. Finally, the staircase ended, and Jhan found himself standing in a spacious open area—circular, to correspond with the forest hollow above—its floor again made from blocks of veiny green marble. Vaguely, it appeared that a huge statue loomed in the very center of this chamber, a heavy silhouetted presence that chilled him, but before he moved closer and shone his light upon it, Jhan tilted back his head and directed his light toward the ceiling.

It was high, and in a couple places teases of sunlight filtered through small chinks where the floor of the bowl had cracked open a little over the years—no doubt from water erosion, because there were wide puddles on the marble floor, though Jhan had noticed a number of rusty metal grates set in the floor, spaced at far intervals, to drain such leakage to someplace even further below. Vegetation hung down raggedly from these ceiling breaches, stringy and dead; plants that had unwisely inverted their growth instead of reaching for the sun.

Jhan walked stealthily toward the center of the chamber, trying not to make a sound, and therefore avoiding the puddles as best he could. He heard a tiny dribbling through one of the floor grates. He was reminded it had rained heavily a couple days ago. Now, as he approached the indistinct massive shadow that formed the nucleus of the chamber, he pointed his phone's light toward it.

When the statue was finally revealed to him, Jhan froze in place, stifling a gasp at its awesome ghastliness.

The statue didn't loom up from the floor…it loomed down from the ceiling, hanging upside down like a bat, the demon lord's membranous wings wrapped tightly around itself like a robe. So, Jhan realized, he was Lord Zon then. Lord Zon, who—according to every grandmother who'd ever read a bedtime story—came from the night skies to snatch away very, very naughty children, to bear them away to work for him as thralls in his cavernous realm…where those children would work until they died, which wasn't very long, after which they would go on working still as damned souls.

This representation of Lord Zon appeared to be made entirely of jade—or else ceramic glazed the color of jade—with touches of gold picking out his jewelry, and traced upon the skin of his wings and body to represent tattoos. His bull-like horns were coated in gold, as were his tusk-like fangs. Upon his forehead, representing another tattoo in gold ink, was that sinister symbol associated with the Ten Demon Lords of Hell...the one that gang kids liked to spraypaint in their territory in Haikan. The symbol that, it was claimed, would be formed when one connected all ten of the temples of the demon lords, if their locations could be discovered. In the center of this forehead tattoo was Lord Zon's third eye. Like his other two, it was gold with a red pupil—the only other color on his being. This third eye, in particular, stared into Jhan's brain like a spear skewered through his skull.

In the light cast from his phone, the third eye's blood-red pupil shifted a little to look even more directly at Jhan.

"No!" he cried out, backing away several steps, bringing up his other arm and burrowing his face into it to crush his closed lids against his eyeballs.

Kai-mo...the dream vine...it was the kai-mo...

"Precious Ruby Empress," he begged in a whisper, almost sobbing, "I will never harm one of your beloved beasts again, I pledge upon my eternal soul! I was planning to leave Uncle's farm soon, after this trip...I swear it! Please, allow me and your faithful follower Mi to escape that life together, and I promise I'll never even put another bite of meat in my mouth so long as I live! Please, just let me find my way out of this forest... Please, just help me get back to Mi!"

When he lowered his arm and opened his eyes, he made it a point not to look directly at the face of the upside down idol of Lord Zon again. This time he took notice of an altar placed on the floor under the inverted statue's head. He dared to draw a little closer to this, though he felt an irrational fear that the enormous stalactite-like mass of the statue might suddenly come loose from the ceiling to fall and crush him. He reminded himself that the ceiling must have been able to support it, somehow, all these many, many years. Maybe the thing was even hollow, its horrifying exterior a mere shell around an empty core...a more impressive version of the fluorescently painted mannikins and papier-mâché demons in the ghost train rides at the Nia-Fa Theme Park, where he had once gone on a class trip. Back then, even those sorry demons had haunted his sleep for days. He recalled now that the bat-winged Lord Zon, much more crudely rendered, had been among them.

Here it was, on the altar: a brass urn filled with sand, into which countless pink-tipped joss sticks had been stuck, though most of these had long ago burned down to stubble. However, four recent joss sticks smoldered, their perfumed smoke rising and twisting like teased-out threads of ectoplasm.

Also atop the lacquered wooden altar table was a brass bowl for offerings of fruit, but the forest fruit had rotted into a foul fermented sludge at which a ring of drunken flies dipped their straws. A corresponding brass bowl contained withered flowers, upon which a few of the drunken flies had alighted to dream. Between the pair of bowls stood a little ceramic cup intended for rice wine, though this was empty. These were kind enough offerings, thought Jhan, never having been in a temple devoted to a demon lord before. He would have expected a platter full of babies' heads…a little cup full of virgin's blood.

As old as the fruit and flowers were, they had still been left here in recent times. Within the past few months? And again…who had lit the incense?

"Hey!"

Jhan whirled toward the voice, holding his phone out at the extent of his arm. Its glow couldn't reach the chamber's enclosing wall. He took a few steps in the direction he thought the cry had come from, but the light still didn't quite reach. A few steps more…unmindful of the puddle he tracked through. His toe accidentally stubbed a bit of fallen rock, or whatever the ceiling was composed of, and it splashed ahead of him.

At this point he could faintly make out the curve of the wall, and he saw that it was pierced at intervals by doorless portals, no light shining from any of them. How many? Judging from the spacing of the two he could now discern, he decided there were ten of them ringing the room. That number made sense. So, just how extensive was this underground structure?

"Hey!" he heard again. The voice was a bit distant, watery with echoes.

He was definitely facing toward the doorway from which the call was coming. A few creeping steps farther. He hoped his light would begin to illuminate the passage's interior.

It's just the dream vine, he told himself, to prevent himself from panicking.

It's a ghost, his mind told him, close to giving in to that panic.

It's a demon…worst of all.

But what if it was…

"Lhop?" he dared to call back, as loudly as his faltering voice could manage.

No answer.

Jhan transferred the carbine from his shoulder to his arms, awkwardly continuing to hold the cell phone with his forward hand as well. He advanced a little more.

"Hey!"

He shuddered. His mind was going to explode, like a clay pot shot by this carbine. His heightening fear caused him to tremble with anger, and his finger coiled against the rifle's trigger.

"Lhop?" he demanded, more loudly.

At the edge of his consciousness, tightening his finger on the trigger made him aware again of the swelling of his right hand. He hadn't checked on that in a while…but now was not the time to do so. Still, its skin felt ballooned, with heat throbbing within that stretched bag. Poisoned…he was simply poisoned by the kai-mo…there *was* no voice…

And in fact, by the time he reached that doorway, the cry hadn't come again.

His light revealed to him a short hallway which opened into a room of as yet indeterminate size, but surely not as large as the great central chamber.

"Hey!" the voice called out from within that room, so much nearer now.

Jhan wanted to shout out a curse. His finger almost jerked back on the trigger, all the way.

"Lhop!" Jhan growled, and he walked boldly into the hallway and to its end.

He'd found Lhop.

First, not far from his feet, he saw Lhop's plastic nose lying on the floor, with its bristling fake mustache attached.

Lhop's body itself lay in a marsh of blood near a narrow bed of moldering wood without a mattress, as if he had rolled out of that bed without even realizing it and slept on the floor after a night in town drinking too much 777 brand beer, Lhop's favorite.

Jhan only recognized this red mass—which glistened in his cell phone's illumination—because of the dislodged plastic nose. Its clothing was shredded, those unbroken areas of its skin so coated in blood that it looked like the entire body had been flayed to the muscles. Ribs showed white, as if licked clean, and a femur too. Thankfully, whatever the corpse might still have for a face was turned toward the wall.

"Oh gods," Jhan was chanting, without even realizing it. "Oh gods, oh gods…"

A doorway at the far end of the room perhaps communicated with another bed chamber, in what was possibly a series of humble cells to house the monks who had apparently once tended this temple. Had they abandoned it, or was it that they'd died out? And if they had all passed away over time, had no one even noticed, or was it just that their role was no longer considered a necessity?

In the doorway to that other room, a dim face began to form out of the gloom, like the disembodied head of some malevolent spirit. A heavy head of striped, moss-colored fur, with a white muzzle dyed red with slathered gore.

"Hey," the face said.

The body supporting the head came with stalking slowness, with the fluid grace of a predator millions of years in the making, tensing up its powerful muscles to spring.

Clever Khup…mimicker of langur monkeys. How many times had Uncle Zep, Aunt Choit, Lhop, and even Jhan himself said "Hey!" to him through the bars of his cage, to get his attention, to assert their dominance over him, to shush his vocal experiments? Had he practiced human speech late in the night, when they'd all been sleeping and he lay in the dark? Uttering this short, remembered sound over and over until he was satisfied? Had it only been for his own amusement, out of boredom, or had Khup hoped to make use of his skill one day?

Lhop had no doubt been the first to fall for his trick.

Jhan didn't ponder these questions now. Upon seeing the face float out of the darkness, his reaction was mechanical and swift. He triggered his carbine three times, in a burst that was almost like automatic fire. With so little space between the tiger and himself, however, he didn't want to remain long enough to fire more, and as soon as the third bullet left the barrel he was spinning away and bolting for the doorway and the circular chamber beyond.

Though it felt like the gunshots in the enclosed monk's cell had blown out his eardrums, through the ringing he was left with Jhan heard the cat's furious roar as it sprang after him.

He tore out into the central chamber, the cell phone's light pointing ahead, bouncing erratically. He was more desperate to keep from dropping the phone than he was dropping the rifle.

He knew he couldn't outrun Khup to the curving staircase, and even if he could have reached the steps before the animal caught up to him, Khup would no doubt have simply raced up them in pursuit. After all, it was by this staircase that the tiger had to have descended into the temple of Lord Zon. No...instead of the stairs, Jhan sprinted toward the altar table at the center of the vast, murky room.

When Jhan reached it, he vaulted atop the lacquered wooden altar, in the process knocking the brass bowl of mummified flowers over the side to crash with a gong. The moment he sprang to the altar top, he was already springing up from it. As he did so, he regretted not taking a second to sling the carbine's strap over his shoulder—but might the tiger have caught up to him if he'd lingered even that long? As it was, he had the cell phone in his left hand, the rifle in his right, and here he was trying to clamber up onto the statue of Lord Zon, projecting colossally down from the ceiling. The toe of his sneaker found purchase in the grooves representing hair at the top of the demon lord's head, but when he tried hoisting himself up onto one of the smooth, gold-painted bull horns, he found the surface slippery and feared he would drop below. In scrambling to secure his hold, he accidentally let go of the carbine.

His reflex was to grip the cell phone all the tighter, its edges digging into his hand. He resisted the impulse, though, of looking below to see where the gun had fallen—whether to the altar or to the floor. Also, he resisted the urge to check where Khup was at that moment. Instead, he concentrated fully on pulling himself up onto the horn, and then stepping onto the less slippery brow of one of Lord Zon's two normally positioned eyes. The brow's shaggy effect made for better footing.

The giant eyeball blazed at him. In the flash of his cell phone light, as he repositioned himself, he saw the pupil was not a giant red gemstone set in place, as he might have wondered, but merely coated in red enamel paint. Paint...a façade...this was no real demon...just an effigy...it would not become enraged that he had desecrated its altar...that he was climbing like a bug upon its visage.

Wherever Khup was in the black void below—which might be as depthless as outer space for all he could tell just then—the cat was not making a sound, neither growl nor imitation of human speech. He could only pray inwardly to the Ruby Empress that the tiger wasn't at that very second jumping up onto the altar table too, preparing to launch itself up onto the face of Lord Zon along with him.

Jhan reached his free hand above him, curled his fingers in the upper rim of one of Lord Zon's nostrils, and pulled himself higher. Huffing with the effort, shaking from terror and the strain, he managed to perch himself on the underside of Lord Zon's nose. Lest the demon lord sneeze him away, he then used the gold-painted tusks curling from the monstrous entity's open mouth to attain an even greater height. He had reached Lord

Zon's maw. Never would he have dreamed that one day he would be grateful to crawl into a demon's mouth, behind its teeth, for shelter.

He was afraid to become cornered in here, however. Originally, he had hoped to fire down at the tiger some more once he claimed a good vantage point, but that was now impossible. If the tiger could catch hold of the statue's face and mount it too, then he would be easy prey. He mustn't stop here! He must keep going…up onto Lord Zon's chin, then up farther onto the folded bat-like wings that enclosed his body, using the finger-like struts of the wings as holds for his fingers and toes. Even if the tiger made it onto the horns, even the chin, there was no way it could follow him up that far…

Still no sounds from Khup. Not even his claws scrabbling at the statue.

But wait…Jhan listened more closely. Before, the sounds of his own huffing breath had masked it…

He thought he heard Khup panting down there.

The sound was far enough below him that Jhan finally dared to lean out from inside Lord Zon's mouth, reach his arm between two fangs, and point the cell phone's light below.

Khup had apparently tried leaping onto the altar top, because the cup for rice wine had been knocked to the floor, and the urn for joss sticks, while still upright, had been pushed almost off the rear edge of the table. Khup, however, lay on his side in front of the altar, breathing heavily. Though the light didn't reach far enough for Jhan to see clearly, he realized then that at least one of the three bullets he had fired in the abandoned monk's cell had struck the jade tiger.

"Hey!" Jhan called down to the animal. "Hey, Khup! I'm sorry, okay?" Now that he saw he had bested the creature, he felt no animosity toward it. He remembered that Mi had given Khup his name. He remembered his vows to the Ruby Empress. "Just go to sleep now, okay?"

He would wait up here until Khup finished dying. He'd curl back into the demon lord's mouth, shut off his cell phone to conserve whatever was left of its battery, and just listen to that panting in the utter darkness until it finally ceased.

Before he could withdraw and shut off the device, however, Jhan noticed movement beyond the dim reach of his smart phone's light.

Two human figures were approaching.

Human *ghosts?*

He could make out their general shape because they brought their own light with them, though it was just as limited as his own, if not warmer in tone. As they came nearer, he confirmed that one of the figures carried a brass lantern with a candle burning inside.

Jhan saw that the pair wore the flowing, sapphire blue robes of monks. Yet, he was perplexed. The head of every monk he had ever seen was shaven bald, at best bearing only a thin stubble, but these two men wore their gray hair long, one with his hair hanging about his shoulders and the other with it gathered behind his head in a ponytail. Both wore thick gray beards besides. Was this look permissible for the unique order of monks who tended the secret temples of the Ten Demon Lords of Hell?

One of the blue-robed monks moved closer to the altar table warily. Jhan had the thought that the monk was going to reverently set the bowl for flowers and the cup for rice wine back in place. He saw, though, the man reach for the fallen carbine, pull it toward him by its strap, and pick it up. Then, the monk backed off a few steps.

Jhan thought he heard the monk mutter something to Khup, where he lay long and beautiful and dying, like a sacrifice to the demon lord himself. Jhan couldn't make out the words. Then, with easy familiarity, the monk raised the rifle and pointed it, and fired one shot through the jade tiger's side and into its heart.

Khup gave a spasm, and by the time the thundering report from the gun had stopped reverberating through the temple's central chamber, the tiger had stopped breathing. With his fanged mouth hanging open, and glassy eyes staring into some other realm, Khup's face much resembled that of Lord Zon himself.

The monk then lowered the rifle, looked up toward Jhan, and gestured for him to come down. He said something too, but Jhan realized he couldn't understand the language the man was speaking.

The other man—he who carried the lantern—stepped closer and called up to Jhan as well. His voice was not demanding or threatening. In fact, he seemed to be trying to sound reassuring. He, likewise, spoke in that unfamiliar tongue.

Or was it so unfamiliar? No...*no*...it *was* familiar, wasn't it? Jhan had heard Western tourists speak in this tongue on his infrequent journeys into Haikan. And many times he had heard this language spoken in foreign movies and shows he'd seen on TV, these programs subtitled with his own country's language.

Jhan was at first afraid to emerge from the mouth of Lord Zon. The tiger's motives he had understood easily...but what might these men do to him? Had they only found these monks' robes, or had they killed the monks for them…killed them so as to make use of this temple for themselves?

Or had the monks taken the two deserters in, decades ago, out of compassion? Might some of those monks live on still, in the deeper catacombs of this temple, after all?

Jhan figured if the aging former soldiers meant him harm, they could easily just point that rifle up here at him and end him now.

At last, Jhan emerged from the demon lord's maw, and carefully climbed down to meet them.

*   *   *

Before the three of them left for their long march through the jungle, both hermits lit a pair of new incense sticks to replace the four in the urn that by now had burned out. They had already returned the fallen flower bowl and ceramic cup to their rightful spots. Jhan watched as the men took the smoking joss sticks and—instead of holding the ends to their foreheads, as he himself would do while praying in one of the temples of the Ten Jeweled Gods—held them pointing out from the sides of their heads as if they were the feelers of an ant…or the horns of a demon. The white men briefly murmured a prayer or some incantation, but rather than it being something learned from monks, Jhan had the impression they were speaking glossolalia, because he didn't recognize the language as being his own, and it also seemed the two men were speaking different words from each other.

Was the ceremony to honor Khup, who they hadn't moved yet from in front of the altar? To honor Lhop, who still lay in one of the monks' cells? Or was this some daily routine, either taught to them or which they had adopted for themselves? Jhan had no way of knowing.

Whatever the case, after their incantations the old men poked the joss sticks into the sand in the urn, and now they were ready to go.

*   *   *

While they hiked along together, Jhan realized he was no longer experiencing the effects of the dream vine. His hand still felt hot, looked red and infected, but later at home the doctor in town would give him a vial of antibiotics. He noticed, though, that the soldier with the ponytail clamped what looked like a cigar in his teeth…until he finally figured out it was a segment of dried kai-mo. Maybe that was why the man grinned at him so much, and whenever the hermit laughed—which was disconcertingly often—it was in a kind of giggle. Jhan imagined it was he whom Lhop's friend had heard down under the hollow in the forest on that long-ago bear hunting excursion.

The two strangers accompanied Jhan to Lhop's truck, and not only did they seem to know where to find it, but it was clear they had been here before. The passenger's side window had been smashed, the cab having apparently been searched for anything useful. In fact, the soldier whose hair fell about his shoulders held out the keys to Jhan.

Jhan just stared at the proffered keys for a beat. Before the three of them had left the temple, this man had to have examined or searched Lhop's body and discovered them.

Jhan gave a shrug, pantomimed turning a car's wheel, and spoke in the language of the Unnamed Country. "I don't know how to drive! I'm afraid I'd crash or something... I can't! I'll have to go on foot." He pointed back down the rutted trail, making exaggerated marching steps.

The two soldiers looked at each other, and the one with the ponytail giggled, held out his hand, and wiggled his fingers. The other soldier relented and handed him the keys.

Before climbing into the cab, the one with the loose hair swiped the pebbles of broken glass into his hand, dumping these into a plastic shopping bag he'd found in the truck rather than litter the ground with them. Then, they were ready to head out.

Jhan sat in the backseat, holding on as best he could as the little box truck bounced along. The soldier driving the truck giggled happily, grinning up at Jhan in the rearview mirror. He had removed the bit of dream vine from his mouth for the time being, vigorously chewing some sticks of gum he had found in Lhop's glovebox.

They didn't take him all the way to his uncle's house, of course—not even to the point where the dirt road became more defined—but when they pulled to a stop it was because they understood it would be easy for Jhan to find his way out of the forest from here. Not a terribly lengthy walk for him, with less likelihood of dangerous animals than deeper in the jungle. Also, not going any further would minimize the chance of anyone spotting the mysterious old men.

The one with the ponytail handed Jhan the keys. This time he accepted and pocketed them. The other one, who had put Khup out of his misery, kept the carbine. From his backpack, Jhan extracted the box with the last five shells, and he offered this to the man. He accepted it with a nod.

"Thank you," Jhan said to them in their language. He had at least picked up that much from movies.

The one with the ponytail giggled in delight and looked at his quiet friend as if proud of a clever son. He popped the cigar-like dream vine back into his mouth, clapped Jhan on the shoulder, and turned away to dissolve back into the forest. The one with the gun gave Jhan an enigmatic look, with weird blue eyes that might reflect spiritual serenity or only a mind blasted mad from war, then followed after his partner.

*   *   *

Out of respect for the men who had led him from the forest, Jhan never told anyone about them. Not even Mi…not even several months later when they lived together in their humble little apartment in Haikan, though they were free now to speak to each other to their hearts' content.

He had told no one—not his sobbing Aunt Choit, not the police who interviewed him—about the temple he had discovered. The temple that Lhop and his uncle had discovered before him. He only said that when the older tiger had attacked them at the base of that ancient tree, he had run off into the forest and become lost. He hadn't witnessed whatever had become of Uncle Zep and his man Lhop.

He lied that the truck's present position was where Lhop had left it, though he said he suspected poachers had broken into it while they were on their excursion into the jungle, because he'd discovered a window was smashed when he'd finally found his way out of the forest. He further claimed that Lhop had given him the keys to keep safe in his backpack.

Jhan was assured by the police that volunteers from town would form a search party, but he hoped the bodies would never be found, lest the forest's long-held secrets be revealed along with them. Then again, he suspected the search would be more a formality than anything, to appease Aunt Choit in return for Uncle Zep's many years of bribes to local authorities.

Hence, Jhan took no credit for the killing of Khup and the larger jade tiger. Mi wouldn't have admired him for it anyway. He didn't want to compromise her growing love for him, which had increased when he had vowed to her that as a follower of the benevolent Ruby Empress, compassionate friend to all animals, he would never allow a morsel of meat to enter his mouth again.

*   *   *

Many a time, in dreams, Jhan would find himself in that subterranean temple again…standing before the altar, sometimes in a t-shirt and cargo shorts, sometimes in a sapphire blue robe, holding two burning joss sticks to the sides of his head like demon's horns.

In these dreams, he would wonder: Did Lord Zon believe his vows, as Mi did? Oh, that far-reaching third eye had seen many a human renege on their oaths, there was no doubt. The Ten Jeweled Gods permitted the demon lord's existence to deal with just such souls.

Lord Zon's fearsome jade visage, viewed upside down in this dank temple beneath the vibrantly alive jungle, gave the impression of wearing a wrathful scowl. But when viewed in the opposite orientation—say, if a photograph of the statue had been flipped around—it would be more obvious that the demon lord was in fact grinning…relishing the pitiful frailties and moral failings of mortals…the ultimate predator, hungry for his prey.

THE FIRST ONES AND THE LAST ONES

-1-

VHEK RECALLED THAT WHEN he was a boy, his mother had told him a story about the First Ones, and he remembered the gist of it even though he had been so small at the time that his sister Jee—six years younger—hadn't even been born.

Just as his mother told the tale to him, the fable began with the Ruby Empress relating a story to Cholukan, the Holy Monkey.

Cholukan had begun his life as a mere pet, but his mistress, the Ruby Empress, most gentle and compassionate of the Ten Jeweled Gods, had assigned the monkey the important role of scribe to the gods. Cholukan was to travel to the mortal realm so that he could report from an earthly perspective—rather than a celestial remove—on the sometimes comical, sometimes tragic, always fascinating doings of human beings. The thought was that as a simian, he was closer to the humans than the humans were to gods.

Cholukan was a yellow-furred macaque, who in place of eyes observed the world through a pair of ruby orbs made from the Ruby Empress' own crystallized tears of blood, after Cholukan—by his very nature mischievous—had, behind his mistress' back, ventured into Hell so as to rescue a gorgeous maiden who'd been kidnapped by demons. Consequently, the sight of Hell had burned out Cholukan's original eyes.

Vhek's mother had already told him the exciting tale of Cholukan's descent into the netherworld, as it was often used to frighten children into not disobeying their parents or anyone else of authority. Though, it wasn't the last time Cholukan—and hence, those who loved hearing about his adventures, or reading about them in books, or watching them on TV—would learn the consequences of letting one's sense of curiosity turn into reckless and dangerous obsession.

*　*　*

"At this time still in possession of his original eyes, young Cholukan was dressed in a blue silken outfit and ready to venture forth into the mortal plane, but before he left, his mistress prepared him with words of advice, which he listened to with his head in her lap, her gentle hand stroking his golden fur.

"She said, 'Beware, my dear little companion, of the mortals you will meet. You are a tricky creature, but they are trickier still. We know that much about them already…all too well. They will mock you. They will hurt you. Because they will not understand you.'

"'All of them, Mistress?' Cholukan asked. For, in changing him from pet to lesser god himself, the Ruby Empress had granted the monkey the power of speech.

"'Not all. But too many.'

"'I will be wary, Mistress.'

"The goddess paused then, as if debating whether to say something further. Finally, as Cholukan turned his head a little to gaze up at her, she said, 'There is another people in the mortal world as well…though, it is perhaps not correct to call them people. Furthermore, I cannot be certain that any of them survive. As you know, from our lofty position in the Ten Realms of Heaven we gods do not see into every shadowed nook and cranny of the terrestrial realm, or else we would not need you to go there on our behalf.'

"'Who are these people who are not people, Mistress?'

"'They are, or were, beings of utter blackness.'"

As a little boy, Vhek had been afraid of the stories—themselves sounding like fables—that there were people in other lands with black skins, thinking they might be either the First Ones or their descendants, but when he had voiced this question his mother had sternly corrected him that the people he referenced were humans just as the two of them were humans, and different only in the way that there were white roosters and black roosters, both equally being roosters. Three decades later, as an adult of thirty-six, Vhek could forgive himself his childhood ignorance. His country had no official name except—when the need arose to refer to it as anything—the Unnamed Country. Even to the point of bearing no name, his homeland had hidden itself as best it could from the rest of the world since the time of the great Emperor Tho, benefitted by the dramatic mountains and dense forests that formed its borders. Thus isolated, its people had remained uneducated about the peoples of other nations, or, indeed, the very existence of most of those nations, until fairly recent times. Of course, nowadays Western tourists visited his country, and living as he did in the capital city of Haikan, Vhek saw them not infrequently. In fact, he enjoyed watching Western movies and TV programs, subtitled into his own language, more than he did the less impressive offerings created by his own countrymen.

"Rather than merely being human beings of a type darker in complexion than other types, the Ruby Empress elaborated, 'The First Ones were as black as the firmament, if the firmament were without stars…as black as ink before it touches paper. My beloved sister, the Ivory Empress—and you as well as I know the greatness of her heart—was the one who eagerly volunteered to sow the terrestrial world with sentient beings who would be our mortal children. Though the Ivory Empress is the youngest of us, with her ten busy hands she had proved to be the most ambitious, and so we all agreed to grant her this wish. Eager as she was, however, and despite her undeniable skills as a creator, she was also rash in the way that the youngest child often is…'"

At this, Vhek's mother had given him a meaningful look, because his sister was still on the way, and being the only child at that time made him the youngest child.

"'Thus, she was more brash than prudent. The Ivory Empress formed the First Ones from the color of the void, black being the absence of color, instead of from the variegated palette of animal and plant life. It was like a child drawing stick men, in that the First Ones were little more than mere outlines. She swears even now that she meant to work on them more later; that they were simply early sketches of her grand design, and we would dishonor my sister by doubting her word. Nevertheless, the point is, she herself admits she made a mistake in releasing the First Ones into the earthly realm prematurely, so as to test them in their future habitat. It was intended only as an experiment. However, as I stress, from our heavenly height we are distant from the mortal plane, and the Ivory Empress quickly lost control of her creations. They scattered, dispersed, and disappeared into the shadows of the world, and into the hours of its night.'

"'Oh, beloved goddess!' Cholukan cried. 'So surely they are still there now? In what numbers?'

"'Even the Ivory Empress isn't certain how many she spawned. But the reason we suspect they may no longer exist is because of the flaws in the design of this proto-race. For one thing, they were not as physically tangible as our human children are. Another flaw was that the Ivory Empress gave them tails, since many animals have them…'

"'Unlike other monkeys, I have no tail!' Cholukan boasted.

"'Shh, naughty monkey, I'm speaking. Giving them a tail was a frivolous touch because, in focusing on such a matter, the Ivory Empress neglected other, more important details. Though they had eyes to see with, the First Ones had no faces and, most importantly, no mouths with which to communicate with each other, and with which to feed. Hence our suspicion that, after all this time, the First Ones have likely died out from starvation.'

"'That is terribly sad,' Cholukan said.

"'Perhaps,' said the Ruby Empress, and she paused again thoughtfully before resuming. 'As I said, the First Ones proved difficult to control. The Ivory Empress confesses that she was not able to instill in them a spark that would grow into benevolence and greatness when they went on to form their civilizations, mere first drafts that they were. She fears that on their own, they would remain bestial. Rumors we hear from the Ten Hells is that even the Demon Lords refuse the souls of those departed First Ones that have appeared at Hell's border, since even the demons profess to be unnerved by them.'

"'Ah, Mistress!' Cholukan exclaimed. 'Then…then perhaps it would be for the best if they have all starved to death, as is suspected. I would very much not want to encounter such beings in my travels in the world of humans!'

"'I doubt that you will, dearest companion. In any case, I certainly hope that you do not. Even if they have indeed all died out, with even the Ten Hells denying their souls entry they may wander the world yet, only in an even less tangible form.'"

-2-

Jee's convent was almost two hours from Haikan, and thus well outside Vhek's normal jurisdiction as a police investigator, but his captain had granted his request to look into the situation his sister had reported to him.

He had never been to Jee's convent before, but he had seen photos of it and even a few videos taken by visitors posted online, and he knew it was situated on a tiny artificial island in the middle of a wide, slow-moving river.

While he waited for the ferry that would bring him to the island, broiling under the noontime sun, Vhek motioned to a woman who tended a stand where they sold coconuts with their green outer husks chopped away. She brought a coconut to him and he paid for it, its top already hacked off and a straw inserted so that he might suck the refreshing water straight from it. Seeing him patronize this woman's business, another woman moved her motorbike closer to him and showed him the plastic bags of water, in which lacy-finned goldfish hovered, that bulged off the bike like some kind of odd nourishment themselves. She asked him if he would like to buy a bag of fish, or perhaps one of the turtles in a covered basket behind her seat, but he declined and looked away dismissively. As he was wearing his uniform, and even had a handgun holstered on his belt, the woman didn't persist as she might have done with someone else, and moved on.

Further down from the wharf where he waited, a water puppet show was underway, watched by a delighted audience of schoolchildren. He couldn't tell which of the Monkey God's many adventures was being portrayed, but even from here he could see that Cholukan was one of the characters being manipulated by the partly submerged puppeteers, and one of the exaggerated voices over the tinny loudspeakers was that of an actor in the role of Cholukan. He was obviously trying to imitate the way the character was voiced in the classic TV series everybody loved and had seen countless times.

The ferry pulled up to the wharf at last, automobile tires hung on its prow and sides to cushion it from bumping. Among the people returning from visiting the nuns' temple were two tourists from some Western country or another. They were ridiculously tall, fit, and tanned, with white-blond hair, more like brother and sister than lovers or spouses, but who could say? Vhek didn't recognize the language they spoke from the movies and TV shows he favored. Well, he couldn't keep up with how many countries there were out there. A little girl who was trying to sell packages of gum to people along the waterfront gaped up at the departing couple as if they were celestial beings that had materialized at the temple so as to then go forth into the material world.

The little girl noticed Vhek watching her and took this as a sign to approach him.

"Buy some gum, sir?" she asked in their language.

"No thank you…it gives me a stomachache."

"You aren't supposed to swallow it, sir."

"I don't swallow it!" he said gruffly. "You swallow your flavored saliva while you chew. I don't care for it. Why aren't you in school?"

"I might be able to afford school if I could only sell more gum, sir."

He considered buying Jee some gum, but what a ridiculous thought. Was she even now a child in his mind, a child forever, his adorable little sister? Thank the gods their situation growing up hadn't been such that

Jee had needed to sell gum or lottery tickets under the blazing sun. Oh well, he'd find someone to give the gum to; one of the officers under his command back in Haikan, probably. He thrust a bill at the urchin, which she only stared at. More gruffly still, he added another bill, and she handed over a single package of gum.

The first people were lining up to board the ferry for its next excursion, and he didn't want to miss out on a spot, so he moved in behind them. The little girl stayed with him.

"What's that on your chin, sir?" she asked with mock innocence.

Smart-mouthed little devil. Shouldn't she save her taunts for those who *didn't* buy her gum? Young men rarely wore facial hair in their country; one seldom saw it until it was gray, at which point beards went without remark. Though he kept his little mustache and connected goatee neatly trimmed, it was not a common look. He himself wondered why he wore it. Perhaps to imitate some of the charismatic actors he saw in those Western movies, in which heroes and villains alike often sported such a look. Perhaps he felt his facial hair afforded him an appearance of wisdom and authority beyond his years, so his underlings and the public, both, would show him a respect that, in moments of insecurity, he wasn't sure he deserved.

"There," he teased the child, "now you can afford to go to school and stop harassing people. Go!"

She saluted him and spun away on her heel like a soldier.

He climbed up onto the ferry, and it was soon leaving the wharf again, with most of its rows of benches empty after all. The only other occupants were a quiet young couple from this country. Maybe they were going to be married soon, and hoped to pray for good fortune at the island temple. They had bought a bag of two goldfish, and the woman carried it on her lap as if it were an external womb. Vhek then considered that they might be expecting and intended to pray to have a healthy child. Seeing him looking their way (Was he always spying on people? Was that the curse of being a policeman?), they both smiled at him shyly. Most police officers in their country wore vividly green uniforms, but his was of a tan color, designating him as an investigator. His epaulets further identified him as a lieutenant. Though he owned a visored cap, even on a bright day like this he preferred not to wear it. Instead, he wore wireframed dark glasses. Maybe another affectation learned from the movies? He sometimes thought he was as much a mystery to himself as those that he was called upon to investigate.

The river was sluggish, brown as mud. Floating alongside the chugging ferry came rafts of fronds fallen from the trees that lined the banks. Trash bobbed alongside occasionally too, and he tossed in his empty coconut. At least his trash was organic matter. When they had gone out a short way, the couple carefully opened their bag of water and poured it over the side, releasing the pair of goldfish for good luck. Smiling to himself, Vhek thought the same two goldfish might very well be caught again, sold again. Bad luck for them.

He was distrustful of the crude boards at his feet, all that separated him from the muddy water beneath them. He hated going out onto water, since he'd never learned to swim. Fortunately, he could already see the island ahead, but at the same time the sight of it made him twitchy. He was almost sorry that the trip to reach it wasn't longer. He hadn't seen Jee since their father's death, four years ago. Since then, their mother had found a boyfriend and gone to live with him. According to their father, their mother had had a boyfriend all along, and in drunken moments he would curse his wife and swear that Jee wasn't his child. On several occasions, that had made Jee cry.

Once, when Jee was twelve and Vhek eighteen, their father downed too many bottles of 777 beer and made that accusation again. Though Jee didn't cry this time, Vhek grabbed his father out of his chair by his shirt, threw him to the kitchen floor, and squatted over him holding to his throat the same knife with which his father had been slicing some mango. Vhek finally let his father up after making him swear he would never say such a thing in front of Jee again. His mother's honor he was less concerned about, being less sure of it, but when they'd been kids he had always been his little sister's protector.

He supposed the gods looked over her these days, that her simple needs were met, and that on her insulated island—an unnamed country within their Unnamed Country—she was safe from the world. If not, he thought, from her memories.

-3-

The temple itself took up just about the whole of the island, which gave one the impression that it would eventually be swallowed by rising flood waters. The building had blue roof tiles, and its outer walls portrayed colorfully painted aquatic themes: fanciful fish, tentacled mollusks with wise eyes, and dragons spouting geysers of water. The ferry slowed and pulled up to the docking platform, where a young novice with a shaven head, wrapped in a blue robe, waited to tie the ferry off and help its passengers disembark. Already Vhek could smell incense on the air.

As the ferry bumped the side of the dock, he realized he had stopped hearing the voice of Cholukan over the loudspeakers a while back. Toward the end of the short voyage to the island, he had begun thinking again of the story his mother had recited to him from memory all those years ago. Obviously, it was what his sister had told him on the phone about her convent's statue of the Ivory Empress that had caused him to remember the tale of the First Ones, and the single time Cholukan the Holy Monkey came close to encountering one of them.

*   *   *

"Cholukan one day found himself walking along a trail through a deep section of forest partway up a mountain, the trail already elevated enough that the air was cooler, the trees cone-bearing rather than tropical. As usual, his only possession was his long walking stick, which also served as his flute and his fighting staff. He had run out of his scant provisions, but the forest always provides if one knows its ways and gifts. The forest can be kind that way, but it can also be cruel. He kept his eye out for jade tigers, black bears, wild pigs, and thieves who might jump unwary travelers.

"Perceptive as he was in this state, Cholukan noticed something odd up ahead, to the right of the trail. Two large trees stood side by side, their trunks of the same girth. The closer Cholukan got to them, the more similar the two trees appeared. Their limbs branched out in an identical way, except in a mirrored image of each other. Even the bark's patterns on the trunks were the same, but reversed. Finally, as Cholukan approached the pair of trees, hooked by his curiosity, he noticed the space between them rippled subtly, like heated air.

"Staring into this space warily, Cholukan was startled when a figure stepped out from behind one of the twin trees—the figure immediately proving to be that of a demon. Cholukan leapt back into a fighting stance and brought his staff before him in both fists, ready to lunge or to counter an attack. However, the demon just stood there in the space between the trees, and Cholukan realized two things. One: he was looking into a secret doorway into the netherworld, perhaps originally created by this demon or others in an attempt to escape Hell into the mortal realm, as some demons will seek to do. And two: the demon was nevertheless unable to step through this doorway, held back by the rippling but otherwise invisible barrier. Either the doorway was flawed and had never been functional, or the demons' plot had been discovered by their superiors and the doorway sealed.

"We humans come in but one form, with minor variations, but demons are like insects in that their wildly varied species run into the millions. This demon that confronted Cholukan through the barrier had a head like a lizard's, but covered in gray feathers, and seemed to be of vast age, with the appearance of having been mummified. Its eyes smoldered with an orange glow like coals, smoke wisping upward from its tear ducts. Its wiry feathered body matched its head, except that the lizard stood upright and was as tall as a man, just like Cholukan. Oddly, the demon was missing its right arm, which ended at a burnt stump just above the elbow.

"'Ho, monkey!' said this ghastly demon. 'I have heard of you! I see by your red crystal eyes that you are the Monkey God who traveled once into my realm, to rescue the virgin Bhi Tu from the demon hags who sought to rob her of her beauty!'

"'I am he,' Cholukan replied leerily. 'And who are you, demon?'

"'My name is of no consequence. Suffice it to say that my function is to stand guard at this portal, so that no demon might try to reopen it to escape into your world.'

"'I see,' said Cholukan. 'I hope you remain successful in that role.'

"'So far I have, but earlier this very day I faced a most unexpected problem. I met a being that was not trying to escape *from* Hell…but *into* it!'

"'What being would want to do that?'

"'A lost and misguided being with no real home of its own. You see, the creature that sought to enter through this portal today was the lingering soul of a First One, who perished I know not when nor how. Perhaps it didn't even realize this portal leads into Hell. Perhaps it saw the trees here on my side, resembling the trees there on your side, and thought it was one of the forests of the Ten Realms of Heaven, rather than being a forest of the Ten Hells. Whatever the case, it tried stepping through the portal.'

"'And failed, I trust?' said Cholukan.

"'Yes, but it was stubborn, this strange unspeaking soul… It kept pushing at the barrier, as if it hoped it would eventually press its way through if it persisted long enough. At first I hung back behind a tree, observing the strange entity, not knowing what to do. However, when I saw that it was not giving up in its efforts, I came out from hiding and approached the barrier to shoo the thing away. That is when this happened.' So saying, the lizard-like demon held up the stump of its right arm.

"'What?' Cholukan said in disbelief. 'It reached through the barrier and seized you?'

"'Yes…it managed to push one limb through, and immediately seized hold of my arm. I cried out at its icy touch and attempted to jerk my arm free of its grasp, but it wouldn't let go. I think it believed it could use me as a handhold to pull itself through. Ultimately, the barrier resisted the First One's efforts, and the thing was repelled. However, it still wouldn't let go of me, and somehow managed to drag my arm through the barrier. When my arm met the air of the mortal plane, I suffered the wound you see now. Have a look by your feet, Monkey God.'

"Cholukan did so, and noticed something that lay in the pine needles before him. It was a slender arm, scaled and feathered, but all scorched and blackened. Its fingers were gnarled like the legs of a dead spider.

"'Monkey God, though I know you owe me nothing, could I nevertheless ask one favor of you? Being the type of demon I am, I am able to regrow my tail or one of my limbs should it become severed. However, I am unable to regrow my arm at present, so long as my severed limb lies out there in your world. Would you, please, insert the limb back through the little tear the First One made in the portal's barrier? On my side, where it belongs, it will rot properly and I will be able to regenerate my arm. In return, I can only offer you one small bit of advice.'

"Cholukan hesitated, considering whether this story might all be some trick on the demon's part, a trap he was being lured into. However, ultimately he decided the demon sounded sincere, and how else had it suffered that amputation? How else might a demon's limb lie here on the earth of the terrestrial realm?

"'Very well,' Cholukan agreed. He lay his staff upon the ground and, repulsed, lifted the severed limb in his hands. He stepped a little closer to the rippling pane between the mirrored trees and studied that space until he detected one small area where the air did not ripple. His monkey nose sniffing, he detected a scent wafting through that little rip that reminded him unpleasantly of his journey into Hell to rescue that ungrateful maiden Bhi Tu, who had cost him his original eyes. Carefully, he aligned the stump end of the severed arm with the tear in the barrier and began feeding the limb into it.

"On the other side, the lizard demon took hold of its limb with its remaining hand, pulling it the rest of the way through. Then, clutching this charred dismembered limb, the demon stepped back, satisfied.

"'I thank you sincerely, Holy Monkey,' said the demon. 'Now, I promised you some words of advice, didn't I?'

"'You did,' said Cholukan. 'And what might those words be?'

"'Run, monkey. That lost soul might still be around here somewhere. Who knows what it might do next. Not even we demons understand the First Ones, alive or dead, if there is even a difference with them. Go, monkey…go quickly.'

"This sounded to Cholukan like wise advice indeed. So he stooped to retrieve his staff, nodded a farewell to the demon on the other side of that odd portal, then turned and continued down the trail at a run…mindful of the shadows between the trees on both sides of the trail as he did so. He didn't stop running, even for a minute's rest, until he finally arrived at a little village, where the villagers welcomed him, and thankfully had no tales to tell of having encountered the lost soul of a First One."

* * *

The nine-foot-tall statue of the Ivory Empress—sculpted from white stone, though small representations of the goddess were often carved from ivory—presided over the tiled courtyard in front of the temple. Vhek might have walked straight over to the figure to give it a look, even before seeking out his sister, but he saw that five of the convent's nuns were making ready to practice a martial arts routine in the courtyard. Vhek cynically assumed they had been waiting for the ferry to arrive before beginning, their synchronized moves more a display for tourists than an exercise in mental and physical discipline. Well, to be fair, surely it was both those things, but already he had spotted one conspicuous donation box near the statue, and he was sure there was at least another box inside, in the shrine hall, along with bundles of incense for sale to those who came to beg favors of the temple's patron goddess.

If they had been expecting a ferry full of tourists this time around, surely they would be disappointed at having to enact their routine for just the three who approached them to watch. Vhek trailed after that couple who had released the bright goldfish to disappear into the murky water that surrounded this place like a great moat.

With their hair grown out only to a stubble, the nuns looked enough alike that not until Vhek had drawn closer did he realize that one of them was Jee.

-4-

Nuns normally wore a blue robe draped over one shoulder, but under that for modesty they wore an outfit of tunic and pants, also blue in color. For the sake of freedom of movement, these five had currently removed that blue outer robe.

Each nun held a blue fan in one hand as they snapped from one pose into the next, flicking the spread fan at the extent of their arms. Vhek had studied martial arts while training to be a policeman, as all recruits were required to do, but their moves had been all business, nothing graceful about them. Mean, street-fighting stuff; how to get a criminal under control and defend oneself from them if they decided to attack, as quickly and efficiently as possible. Vhek had to admit, he was already impressed by these agile women with their forceful yet elegant movements, and their stoic, set expressions.

He might have mistaken them for men at first, and later he would find that one of them had indeed been born a male. Such a person, who held the conviction that their soul was of the opposite gender, was accepted in their culture as an "accidental woman" for having been born into the wrong body. Another of the five looked to be in her early fifties, but her movements were just as fluid as those of the younger nuns. And Jee... He had seen her once before with her hair shorn, and in the vestments of a nun, at their father's funeral, but it was another thing to see her here at this temple where she lived, going through these martial arts exercises. This was his funny, mischievous little sister? So afraid of her nightmares that one night she had begged to sleep in his bed, and thereafter had ended up sleeping in his bed every night for the next few years, despite their parents' disapproval? Look at her now...look at her firm expression, her grave eyes.

When the performance—as Vhek still irreverently thought of it—was over, the young couple offered compliments, and the older nun bowed slightly in thanks. Vhek took her to be the abbess, because she looked his way and nodded meaningfully. She set off to return to the temple with three of the other nuns, leaving Jee to walk toward him.

As she came, behind her Vhek saw the young couple trailing after the nuns into the temple. He was fine with not joining them at the altar, because he had no prayers to offer. He had never been devoutly religious, nor even very superstitious. Superstition was for scary bedtime stories.

"Brother," Jee said, smiling reservedly.

Vhek wanted to hug her, actually had to catch himself from doing so. It wouldn't be seemly to embrace a nun, would it? Even if she was one's own flesh and blood.

"Very impressive, Jee," he told her, also smiling in a polite way, as if meeting her for the first time. He couldn't help but feel uncomfortable with her. Would that ease up gradually? Could it? "Your fighting techniques."

"They aren't really fighting techniques."

"Oh no? You don't practice with weapons like swords and lances?"

"Well…yes, we do those things."

"And you don't study unarmed methods of defending yourselves and innocent victims, in case of attack?" At a loss with how to connect with her, he went straight to teasing her, in imitation of their childhood.

Her smile grew just a bit. "We do."

"And isn't every monk and nun in our country prepared to fight as a warrior if our land is ever invaded by foreigners?"

Now her smile was such that she actually showed a glimpse of teeth. "It's good to see you, Vhek. Thank you for agreeing to come."

"I'm happy your abbess was amenable to it, as my captain was."

"Are you thirsty?" she asked.

"No, I had something a short while ago. Thank you."

"Very well. Then…why don't I just show you what I called you about." She pointed past him, toward the statue of the Ivory Empress.

"Let's do it," he said.

As she walked beside him, he smelled years of incense impregnated into the very weave of her garments, maybe into the cells of her flesh, and he caught the scent of her sweat too. Why should one individual's sweat seem familiar to him? It was all in his mind. Then again, he had heard of something called pheromones. Could one be recognized from that mysterious substance? Weren't pheromones given off to arouse sexual feelings in others? Like her pretty face, with its striking dark eyes, and her attractive form, it was an unnecessary mechanism in this life she had chosen. All of these were animal attributes, material baggage; only her womb could be of less importance to her. Unlike her personal belongings accumulated over the years, these things could not be sold, given away, or destroyed. At least she had shorn off the long black hair that he still pictured whenever she appeared in his thoughts.

He knew too well that being desired, being seen and acted upon as some object of passion, was the prime reason she had come to live this life, insulated on this island.

The statue of the Ivory Empress, sitting cross-legged atop a pedestal in the stylized form of a lotus flower, loomed taller over the siblings as they approached it. Nine of the goddess' bared, slender arms extended from her torso, radiating like spokes, with the tenth arm folded in front of her chest, its hand cocked upward between her breasts as if to mark the central pathway of the goddess's body. Much was made of the body's meridians of energy in their beliefs, and of the symmetry seen in the human form and elsewhere in nature. Symmetry equated harmony. Gazing up at the statue, taking in its design and symbolism, Vhek was reminded of the portal in the woods Cholukan discovered: the two trees, identical but reversed, indicating the uneasy but crucial balance between the Ten Heavens and the Ten Hells.

In the case of any statue of the Ivory Empress, the only variance in its symmetry should be that tenth arm folded across its chest, but of course there was a reason for that. With this hand, the goddess indicated *herself.* The other nine hands typically held objects representing the other nine Jeweled Gods. The always eager, helpful, busy-handed Ivory Empress gathered the blessings bestowed upon humanity by her brothers and sisters, and offered them to mortals, volunteering as a kind of emissary between the eternal and earthly realms. In the case of these proffered objects, there would still be symmetry of shape, though not of color. Each upturned hand was to hold in its palm a glass or ceramic orb, tinted or glazed the color of the auspicious gemstone that represented that particular god.

Hence, the five arms sprouting from the right side of the goddess' body should bear spheres that symbolized the Jade Emperor, the Diamond Emperor, the Sapphire Emperor, the Topaz Emperor, and the Garnet Emperor.

In the hands on the left, excluding the tenth, should rest spheres that represented the Ruby Empress, the Pearl Empress, the Opal Empress, and the Quartz Empress.

The problem was—and Vhek had spotted this even before approaching the statue—that the orbs that should rest in the four hands on the Empress' left side were missing, pried or broken from the sculpted palms into which they had been fixed.

"If it was just one ball," Jee said, "we might believe it had fallen away on its own, loosened over time…that maybe it rolled away somewhere. Maybe even into the water. But *four*…"

"Why would someone do this?" Vhek said, wagging his head. His expression was intense enough that an observer who knew him to be a policeman might grow afraid. Even though he was not religious, this vandalism struck him as sacrilegious. It offended his sense of cultural pride, his sense of law and order, and his sense of…balance. "Surely there can't be a single person in the whole of our country who would think those spheres, in themselves, had any monetary value. I can only imagine some street rat doing this on a dare, maybe as part of a gang initiation rite, though I've never known even punks to do such a thing." He turned to Jee. "No one heard anything?"

"No, Vhek. In the morning, we came out to sweep and mop the courtyard, and that was when Sister Kwen noticed it."

"And you have no security cameras?"

"No, none. Why would we?"

"Aren't you afraid someone might steal the donation box out here?"

"We empty it every night before retiring."

"So no one heard a boat motor?"

"I told you, we heard nothing. They must have used oars."

Vhek stared at the statue again through the lenses of his sunglasses, which distorted the hues of the remaining five orbs. Why had *those* been left? His instincts told him it had been done to purposely create a sense of disharmony, but his instincts didn't tell him *why*.

Wearing an ornate headdress, the Ivory Empress with her youthful and lovely countenance gazed off into the distance serenely, as if unperturbed, trusting these human children to resolve the issue for her.

Vhek muttered, "This is most strange."

"And that's why I asked to bring you here."

"Well, it is a serious matter. Like I say, not so much in terms of stolen valuables, but in the sense that this is a vile desecration."

"It's a blasphemy," Jee said grimly.

"Do you women have any enemies? I've heard of foolish rivalries that develop between one monastery and another—a few that even resulted in violence."

Jee hesitated in replying, long enough for her silence to be significant, and Vhek looked at her again. When their eyes met, she said, "Well…there might be something almost of that nature."

-5-

Jee had awakened screaming.

Her cries were so loud, so desperate, that Vhek thought an intruder had stolen into their home under cover of night and was attempting to assault the eleven-year-old in her bed. So shrill, so frantic her cries, he thought perhaps she was even being stabbed to death.

Vhek, then seventeen, leapt from his bed and across the short hallway to his sister's room. Since there were just the two children, they had their own bedrooms to themselves, with their parents in the third bedroom here on their little house's second floor. Vhek tried to twist the knob of Jee's door, but it was locked. As he jiggled the knob and called Jee's name, his parents crowded behind him, also startled from sleep. His father was cursing.

Vhek was just about to slam his shoulder into the flimsy door when it opened, and there stood Jee in her faded, rumpled pajamas. Her face was contorted with misery, her long black hair mussed from sleep, with strands sticking to the tears on her cheeks.

"What is it?" their mother asked, pushing past Vhek to look at the girl sternly.

"A dream is what it was," their father said, already returning to his room. "Fuck!"

"Someone was standing at the foot of my bed!" Jee sobbed. "I thought it was Daddy... I called out to him, but he didn't say anything...he just stood looking at me!"

"Your father was in bed with me!" their mother said angrily. "It was a dream, like he said!"

"Even if it was a dream," Vhek said, "why do you have to yell at her? Can't you see how afraid she is?"

"Because she almost gave me a heart attack," their mother snapped, starting to turn back to her room after her husband. "Go back to sleep!"

"Nobody loves me... *nobody!*" Jee wailed.

"Shh, come on," Vhek said, stepping forward to put his arm around her shoulders. "Don't say that. You just scared them, that's all."

"They're not as scared as me!"

"Oh stop, foolish girl," their mother said, while closing her bedroom door.

In a low voice, Vhek said to his sister, "She calls you foolish, but she filled our heads with spooky bedtime stories all our childhood. When we sleep, there they are, like a library of nightmares to choose from." He smiled, trying to calm her down with a touch of humor.

"Vhek, can I sleep in your bed?" Jee said, still miserable.

He sighed. When she'd been even younger, a toddler, she'd been all over him constantly, making him feel suffocated. He was only eight himself when she would insist on sitting on his lap as they watched Western cartoons on TV. Irritated, Vhek would complain to his mother, and she'd reply, "But she loves you!" Sometimes little Jee would want to nap with him in the steamy heat of afternoon, and she always snuggled up right against him, making him even more uncomfortable, so he would push her body away from his, only for her to cuddle close to him again soon enough, all this without her even waking up. But he was older now, more patient, and if he didn't comfort her, who would?

"All right, come on," he told her.

"At least *you* love me, Vhek."

In the dark of his room, under his quilt with him, she drew close but at least didn't spoon with him, her ankles simply resting across his. They lay on their backs, both staring at the dark pool of the ceiling, feeling the cool air of the standing fan his parents had finally bought him breeze against their faces. Sensing her eyes were open, Vhek whispered, "Go to sleep."

"When I screamed," Jee whispered back to him, "I saw the person disappear. That was when I knew it wasn't Daddy."

"It's like they said, Jee, it was only a dream."

"It didn't feel like one. I woke up…maybe because I felt it there watching me. I was *awake!* It was a ghost, I think, Vhek."

"If a ghost haunted our house, one of us would have seen it before. Our family has lived here since before you or I were even born, and I've never heard our parents say a ghost lived here." He chuckled as he repeated his own words. "A ghost *lived* here."

"You've never seen anything like that?" Jee insisted. "A shadow in your room you thought was watching you, and then it faded away when it saw that you saw it?"

Vhek was going to tell her of course not, but a memory came back to him before he could speak. Something he had forgotten, or made himself forget.

He had, in fact, on one occasion awakened to the feeling that there was a presence in his room. Later he would be certain, absolutely certain, his eyes had been open. That it hadn't been a dream…just as Jee said now.

Jee was only a baby then, so he must have been six, or would it be seven? In any case, it wasn't so very long after the story his mother had told him about Cholukan meeting that demon in the forest, standing at the threshold of a portal to Hell. A demon missing one arm.

The presence he thought he just barely detected in the gloom of his bedroom was a hunched shape beside his bed, like a large dog. They had owned a dog at that time, but it wasn't allowed into their bedrooms, not even onto the second floor, and it was just a small scrawny mongrel anyway.

The shape lifted an indistinct head above the line of the bed, and that was when Vhek felt he could make out two dim eyes in its otherwise empty face. Eyes that were more human than dog-like…as if a man had crawled close to his bed on hands and knees.

And yet, the half-hidden figure also seemed to have a long, thick tail drooping behind it.

Vhek had jerked his quilt up over his head, too terrified to call out for his parents. As if hoping the thing right there beside him hadn't seen him, but of course it had. Surely it heard him whimpering under his worn old quilt too.

Finally, he summoned the courage to peek out from under his quilt, because he couldn't just wait forever until the dark figure did…whatever it had come to do, could he?

He hadn't heard it move while he had been hiding under his quilt, and that was no doubt because when he finally did peek, he saw nothing there beside him in the murk. No figure on all fours, with a tail at one end and those barely discernible eyes at the other.

He scrambled out of bed and flipped the switch to turn on the ceiling light. He didn't care if he got in trouble should his parents discover he had done so, but with his door closed they weren't aware, and he slept with that light on for a whole week—without further incident—until he finally felt brave enough to risk the darkness again.

He never did see that skulking shape again, but now Jee's nightmare struck him as eerily similar. Well, he thought, it was surely a universal fear: some mysterious stranger watching you from the shadows. It was probably an illusion rooted in animal memory; a survival instinct from prehistoric times, when humans sheltered in caves from saber-toothed jade tigers. When every shadow might have murder on its mind.

Seventeen-year-old Vhek whispered to Jee, "Did Mama ever tell you the story of Cholukan meeting a demon who was attacked by one of the First Ones?"

"Yes!" she hissed emphatically. "Oh, yes! Vhek…you don't think it was a First One who came to steal my soul, do you? They don't have souls like us, so they try to drink ours until they have enough soul in them to get into the Ten Heavens. Or at least into the Ten Hells, because they hate having nowhere to go when they die!"

"No, no, *no*," Vhek told her, "I don't think that at all. I still think it was just a dream. All I mean is, like I said before, Mama has filled our heads with all of Cholukan's scariest adventures, and then she complains when you have a nightmare."

"Anyway, Vhek, can I sleep in your bed again tomorrow night if I'm still nervous?"

He wanted to groan wearily, because he cherished his privacy. Alone in the dark was his time to think of beautiful girls from school, or Western movie actresses, and indulge the powerful hungers of his teenage body, but how could he say no when his sister appealed to him for his protection in such a pitiful way?

"Of course," he sighed. "Whatever you want. But just go to sleep now, all right? We have school in the morning."

Jee leaned close to give him a quick kiss on the cheek, which surprised him, as he couldn't recall her ever having kissed him before. He couldn't recall *anyone* ever having kissed him, unless his mother had done so when he was too young to remember. He thought it was cute; it warmed him. It was reward enough for his gallantry. Jee then lay back, became silent, and soon dozed off. Listening to her breathing, he lay awake a little while longer, staring again at the ceiling's inky pool.

He was glad he had never told Jee about the shape he'd seen beside his bed years earlier…and he kept that secret thereafter.

-6-

"Do you remember," Jee asked him, "that story Mama told us when we were little? About the First Ones?"

"Funny you should say that," he replied, with a little laugh. "I was thinking about it on the ferry just now."

Jee's dark eyebrows gathered intensely. "Yeah? And why was that?"

"Oh, just because of the statue…the Ivory Empress. It reminded me of how she sent the First Ones into the world, only to regret it."

Jee nodded at this, but still looked severe, as if she thought there might be more to the coincidence than this.

They sat upon a lacquered bench carved from one heavy piece of wood, in a little hallway off the central shrine area. Her quarters were in a dormitory wing just beyond this hallway, she had told him, but she was not permitted to bring even a male family member there. She had given him a can of white fungus drink, and this time he accepted her offer. With the martial arts drill finished, she had donned her azure robe.

"Well," Jee continued, "we're aware of a group—you would call them a cult—of people who are fixated on the First Ones. They consider them our true forebears, and they…I almost said they worship them, but that isn't quite right. They try to summon them though, to commune with them…I'm not sure how. Through prayers, through rituals maybe. Seances or dark magic. These people still believe in the Ten Jeweled Gods, and acknowledge that the gods are the creators of the universe and all it contains, but they rebuke them. It's my understanding that they even curse the gods for turning their backs on their original children, the First Ones, and subsequently abandoning them to a kind of limbo."

"So, are they demon worshippers then?"

"No, Vhek, did you hear what I said? It's the First Ones they're obsessed with, not demons."

"All right, I get it. Well, their sympathy toward the First Ones sounds misguided, if it creates such resentment in them. These cultists might very well resent a statue of the Ivory Empress, who designed the First Ones…enough so to deface it."

"That would seem to be the most likely explanation."

"But I've never heard of such a cult before."

"They don't advertise themselves, do they? Most people would be enraged by their attitude toward the gods. So, because they're secretive, I don't know how widespread they are."

"Do they have a name for themselves?"

"Yes. It's our understanding they call themselves the Last Ones."

"Huh. Well, since you've heard of these Last Ones before, do you know if there are any of them in this area?"

"Mother Xo has spoken to us about them. She says there are."

"Could I speak to Mother Xo about this myself?"

Jee stared at her brother for a moment, considering his request, and finally said, "Let's find out if she's awake…and if she'll see us."

*   *   *

Vhek was confused. Awake? Wasn't the abbess that woman in her fifties who had joined in the martial arts drill and nodded to him? He asked Jee this as they went toward Mother Xo's quarters, in the dormitory wing—away from any visitors, away from recorded chants and gongs played over hidden speakers. No, no, Jee replied, that hadn't been Mother Xo.

They were accompanied by a beautiful young nun Jee had introduced as Sister Kwen, the one who was an "accidental woman." When Kwen was out of earshot, Jee had confided in Vhek that Kwen was a former bar girl who had escaped from that sad existence to pursue a spiritual life.

What Jee didn't add was the similarity between Kwen and herself, since she, too, had fled from animal desires.

Kwen's main responsibility at the temple was tending to Mother Xo's personal welfare, and so Jee had consulted with Kwen about an audience with Mother Xo. Kwen had checked to see if the abbess was indeed awake, returned to report that she was—and was willing to meet with the police investigator—and now Kwen led them to the abbess's room.

"Mother," Kwen said, stepping into a small, gloomy chamber ahead of Jee and Vhek, and bowing deeply. "Here is the brother of Sister Jee, to humbly ask you some questions."

Beyond Kwen, Vhek heard a small croak, a half-voice almost empty of air. At this sound, Kwen stepped aside, allowing Jee and Vhek to move into the room.

Jee bowed deeply as Kwen had done. After a moment of shock at the sight of the abbess in her bed, Vhek himself bowed. He couldn't remember the last time he had bowed to anyone. As he did so, he managed to get out, "Thank you for agreeing to see me, Mother Xo."

He had never seen anyone so old, so withered, so frighteningly emaciated, who could still draw breath. He didn't understand how the organs within this mummified body before him, its skin a literal bluish-gray, could still be functioning. The ancient nun's limbs, where they extended from her blue robe, were mere bones, her skull thinly painted with skin. Still, from inside the caverns of her eye sockets, her milky eyes seemed to take in Vhek with clarity. Somehow, the memories of long-vanished muscles in her right arm allowed her to lift it so as to point to a wooden chair behind him.

"Please sit," the nun whispered in her ghostly creak.

"Thank you, Mother," Vhek said, still in awe of this ghastly but remarkable creature, this sentient cadaver. He sat on the heavy lacquered chair as invited, while Jee and Kwen remained standing.

"Mother Xo," Jee said, "my brother Vhek is the police lieutenant who has kindly come to look into the matter of our desecrated statue. Though he is receiving his usual salary for this work, he was told he must use the vacation time he has accrued in order to take time off from his regular duties."

"That is very commendable of you, young man," Mother Xo said, nodding her head. She was propped up with pillows, almost into a sitting position. "We greatly appreciate you using your personal time to come to our assistance."

"Even if I can't resolve this issue in the two weeks I have at my disposal," Vhek said, "I vow to come here on my two days off every week, if I have to, until I see the matter to some kind of conclusion."

"You are a man of devotion," Mother Xo said.

Vhek didn't know if she meant he was devoted in a religious sense. He was not. Hoping she wouldn't pursue that avenue of discussion, he simply thanked her for the compliment, then went into his first question. "Mother Xo, my sister told me there is a kind of cult of misguided souls who venerate the First Ones of legend..."

Mother Xo cut him off immediately, raising that same gnarled claw again. "The First Ones are not legend, young man. They are not mere myth. They are a reality."

"Yes, Mother," Vhek said. He wondered if this was a waste of time. This woman had lived for—how long?—outside the commonplace world, the world of jobs and paying bills and raising children, absorbed only in chants and incense and fanciful tales of ten-armed goddesses, believing that the adventures of Cholukan the Monkey God were factual accounts. He himself hadn't believed in the latter since he was a teenager.

"No one is wiser than Mother Xo in these matters," young Kwen said proudly, as if to further convince Vhek of the abbess's statement. "She is one hundred and twenty-three years old."

"Oh my!" Vhek said. If someone had told him this without him seeing her, he wouldn't have believed it. He believed it.

"This is the last year of my mortal life," Mother Xo told him.

"What? Vhek stammered. "Why? Are you..." He didn't want to say "dying." Of course she was dying; she looked like she had been dying before he was even born. Well, all of them here in this room were dying. Sloughing off their mortal vessels in daily increments, like the falling dust of shed skin cells.

"One, two, three," Mother Xo explained. "It is the auspicious number of my final year."

"I see," Vhek said, though he didn't. If her prediction didn't come to pass before her one hundred and twenty-fourth birthday neared, would she poison herself? Refuse food? Maybe just will herself to expire? He believed she could do that, since it looked like she had willed herself to remain living in this all-but-dead husk for decades.

"You want to know about the Last Ones," Mother Xo said. "They are a reality. And you are correct...they are misguided. Their pity for the First Ones would be commendable, were it not for their disdain for the Ten Jeweled Gods. They are vengeful; their minds have become distorted. The Last Ones contend that the First Ones are not simply unfinished sketches, best left discarded. They believe that the First Ones in their uncompleted state are actually more *pure* than human beings for being in that state. Like the beasts of the forest, they are thought to be simpler, less corrupted, less sinful than human beings. And thus, to the Last Ones, actually superior."

"I see what you mean about a distorted view. Now that I understand their beliefs, though, I'd like to know where I might find them, in order to look into their doings. Are they an organized group? How many of them are there...and where? Have you ever seen or even met any of them, during your long life?"

"I may have seen them, even met them, without ever knowing it. You might have done the same, young man. I cannot tell you numbers, but I don't believe they are great. However, they do seem to be dispersed throughout our country. And there appears to be a small group of them close by, in town."

"If I might ask, how do you know that, Mother?"

"I have seen that group in dreams."

Oh boy, thought Vhek. Listening to Mother Xo speak with such apparent knowledge on the subject, his hopes for being able to investigate this cult had been rising. Now those hopes all but crashed. *Dreams?* He tried to conceal the disappointment in his voice when he said, "Oh? And can you tell me of these dreams?"

"I have had them repeatedly, more frequently in recent years. In the dreams, I see a group of people...perhaps a half dozen. The number seems to vary, and I don't see the individuals clearly. They meet in a house or small building in town. In my dream visions, the Last Ones enact strange rituals that unsettle my astral presence. Their rituals are sometimes successful in calling a First One, or even a number of First Ones, to appear. At that point, I always wake up, unnerved—because the First Ones turn to look at me with those eyes of theirs, that glow in their black faces."

"They...*see* you in your dreams?"

"Yes. The Last Ones never notice me...but the First Ones do."

Vhek heard Sister Kwen mutter to herself, perhaps a protective blessing.

"You once saw a First One yourself, Mother Xo, didn't you?" said Jee. "In the waking world?"

"I did," said the abbess.

"Really?" Vhek said. Though he was still disappointed that the Last Ones might only be a figment of Mother Xo's imagination after all, he had to hear this story...if only to compare it to the nightmares he and his sister had experienced many years ago. So he said, "Could you tell me about that, if you would, Mother Xo?"

-7-

"A hundred and thirteen years ago, no foreigners had yet come to set foot within our country, as it still lay unknown except to the neighbors who directly border us, but at that time a person might still encounter one of the last surviving First Ones in their physical form. Such as it was.

"I had four brothers and three sisters, and every day in good weather all of us would be out in the rice paddies, along with our parents and aunts and uncles, squatting down barefoot in the muddy water, plucking out clumps of bright green stalks…all of us joking and chattering and gossiping. We had no TV, no internet, nor even telephones, such as you have now, and we were no poorer for it. We worked hard, yes, but my family was healthy and loving. Heh…and here I am now, these many years later, having to be spoon-fed rice porridge by my dear Kwen, as if I've returned to helpless infancy!

"We didn't go to school, but our parents and grandparents taught us practical skills, and shared their knowledge of our history and culture, as did the monks at our temple. Not this temple here, mind you. I'll tell you why not, in a moment…

"We also learned through observation of the land we were so connected to, with all its plants and animals, and the expressions of the weather. As hard as we worked, we also found time for play, but because we played mostly outside, linked to our play was this discovery of nature.

"A boy who lived nearby started coming around often to see my sister Chot, who was fourteen at that time and becoming quite the beauty. Well, she was always beautiful from earliest childhood, was Chot. Bless her! She grew ill and died at only twenty-three; can you imagine? A hundred years younger than I am now. I would gladly have given her half the years of my own life if I could have seen into the future and gifted her so.

"In any case, this boy was ever trying to impress Chot with silly acts of bravado, stupid jokes, big stories. My brothers and other sisters and I were always entertained by his antics, though I could tell my parents were rather less amused by his disruptive visits. As I was saying, he told grand stories, and told them loudly, as if he were some worldly traveler, and one afternoon he told Chot an especially curious story. As we all worked together closely, the rest of us couldn't help but listen in. This boy—his name was Fanh—Fanh said that while helping his uncle gather mushrooms in the forest, they had chanced upon an odd little monument, almost like a gravestone, planted in the ground close to a tree. As the tree had grown, it had tipped this monument at an angle. His uncle claimed to have once found a monument just like it, except that one was so close to a tree that the tree had grown around it, so that the monument was half absorbed inside the trunk. Supposedly, there are more of these monuments scattered throughout our country's forests, but most of them are now completely concealed inside tree trunks. Occasionally, I've heard, lumber workers have broken their saws on them. They refuse to use the wood from any such tree.

"The purpose of these miniature monuments was unknown, but some people whispered that they had been created by the First Ones, and though no one truly understood their significance, there were various theories. Some dismissed them as ancient property markers. Because of their phallic shape, others surmised they were ancient fertility symbols. Others, though—those who attributed them to the First Ones—had far more bizarre interpretations.

"Now, on an earlier occasion, Fanh had related a story about this same uncle, who was known to indulge too much in rice wine, so his stories were admittedly suspect. But supposedly, when he himself had been a teenager, this uncle and a friend had discovered in the forest the body of a First One that had only recently died. It hadn't been killed by an animal, as it bore no apparent marks of violence, and it is said that no animal will feed on the corpse of a First One. However, the body they found was rotting before their eyes, rapidly, as if it were liquifying. They said there was no stench of death, but the uncle and his friend covered their noses and mouths anyway, afraid to breathe in the air near the thing. They described it as a mostly shapeless mass, hairless and blacker than the night sky, and said if it had any limbs they were either tucked up under the body or had already dissolved. All that remained was the head on one end, and a long tapering tail at the other. They saw no eyes, though they may have been closed or facing down into the ground. The boys poked this mass with sticks, and the sticks sunk right into it, as if it were gelatin. They soon left to go get the uncle's father so that he might see the body for himself, but by the time they returned with the man the thing had entirely melted away, and the uncle was taken for a liar by even his own father.

"Overhearing this story, and seeing how we children stared at Fanh in wide-eyed horror, my father yelled at the boy and told him to stop trying to frighten us with foolish stories, and to go away and let us get on with our work.

"So when Chot asked if she might accompany Fanh into the forest to see this monument for herself, my father grew angry, and looked ready to send Fanh away again, but my mother spoke softly to him. My mother was beautiful herself, and always had her way with my father. Whatever she whispered to him, he then said to Chot, 'You can go with Fanh…but only if you take your brothers and sisters with you.'

"'Oh, Daddy!' my sister said, and the rest of us all giggled.

"'You heard me, Chot! And, Fanh…if one of my children is killed by some tiger in the forest—if one of them comes back with anything more than a scratch—I'll gut you alive, then impale you on a post as a scarecrow, do you hear me?'

"After we finished working for the day, we set out for the forest, and my two oldest brothers brought sickles with them…moreso to intimidate Fanh, I'm sure, so he wouldn't try touching beautiful Chot, than to defend the rest of us from any forest animals!

"It was late afternoon, and my father further warned us that we'd better get back before it grew dark, or else. 'I'm going to start sharpening a stick to skewer you on, just in case I need it,' he advised poor lovesick Fanh.

"So we marched away, the eight of us and Fanh, laughing and excited. Hearing such a clamor as we entered into the woods, no dangerous animal would have dreamed of approaching us.

"We went farther and farther into the forest, until I grew afraid that we'd become lost, but Fanh seemed confident that he knew the way. He reassured us of this by pointing out some landmarks as we got closer to the place we sought. Finally, to my relief, he announced that this was the spot. He proudly indicated an old banyan tree with an immense trunk, and there between two of its roots stood a small monument, indeed like a gravestone, slanted at an angle.

"The stone came up to about Fanh's hip. It was rough in texture, pitted with age, and spotted with lichen…cylindrical in shape, with a rounded top. There were no inscriptions or features except for two elliptical openings, shallow in depth, chiseled beside each other near the top of the stone. Clearly, these indentations were meant to represent eyes.

"Fanh stepped aside to let us inspect the stone, and we swarmed upon it. My youngest brother laughed and slapped the top of it, as if it were the head of an even smaller child. Another brother stuck his fingers into those two eye holes to an outburst of general amusement. I myself hung back, however. A strange, unseen aura seemed to emanate from the monument that apparently no one else in our party picked up on. Perhaps they simply didn't want to admit to sensing it, and thus potentially invite ridicule. In fact, I think my siblings' comical antics were partly a show, to convince the rest that they weren't afraid. To convince *themselves* that they weren't afraid.

"My oldest brother became quite naughty in an effort to outdo all the others. He lay on his back spreadeagled, with the monument rising from his groin area. Chot scolded him, but she was laughing too, and when my brother pretended to moan, Fanh laughed so hard he had tears in his eyes.

"Suddenly, my oldest brother's expression changed completely, from mock ecstasy to wide-eyed horror. Lying on his back as he did, he had spotted something above him. Before he could even cry out, I darted my eyes to the heavy limbs that spread widely above our heads from that monstrous tree.

"I saw it for only an instant, but it was not a trick of the light—I knew it then and remain convinced now. Yes, there was a play of sunlight through the canopy of the banyan tree, and a breeze stirred the leaves and hence their shadows. But no trick of light could account for the two human-like eyes I saw gazing directly down at me from a mask of utter darkness. In fact, those eyes made direct contact with mine.

"My brother was already babbling frantically, and scrambling to his feet, when I let out a scream of my own.

"There was such chaos then, so many confused and frightened voices, that they masked whatever sounds the First One might have made in the branches above us. Its head had ducked away only a fraction of a second after our eye contact, and the creature had either flattened itself to the massive bough it perched upon, or had leapt higher into the tree to conceal itself in the shadows. Whatever the case, it was gone. But those eyes. I can see them still...

"My youngest brother was sobbing, pulling at Chot's sleeve, begging her to take us home. She in turn demanded that Fanh bring us back immediately. He didn't protest.

"Along the return journey, we looked over our shoulders constantly, to be sure we weren't being followed. Fanh said to my oldest brother, 'Are you certain what you saw wasn't a baby bear, hiding in the branches? Their faces are black.'

"'It had no face!' my brother insisted. 'You don't believe what I saw, and yet you were convinced the First Ones planted that monument there?'

"'But...but,' Fanh said. 'I...I didn't really believe it one hundred percent!'

"'Well, now you can!' said my eldest brother.

"'We shouldn't tell father,' said Chot. 'He'll be angry!'

"'But why should he be angry?' Fanh said.

"'He'll think we're lying,' said another of my brothers. 'That would make him angry.'

"'You're right. He'll just say I was mistaken,' my eldest brother agreed.

"You might wonder why I didn't speak up—then or later—to corroborate my brother's story...to say I had witnessed the First One too. I'm not sure why. I think I was simply too afraid to admit it. If I did, it would make things more *real*. More certain. Nor did I want to add to my siblings' fear. Later, when they asked why I had screamed that way, I said it was because my brother's panicky cries had startled me.

"I never did tell my siblings or my parents what I saw up there in the branches of that banyan tree. But not only did my siblings and I never venture again to that deep section of the forest...it is my understanding that Fanh refused to ever go mushroom gathering with his uncle again."

-8-

"Do you believe my story, young man?" Mother Xo asked Vhek in her cracked and hissing voice at the conclusion of her story.

"Yes, Mother," he told her.

"And what Fanh's uncle found when he was a boy? Those decaying remains?"

"Him I can't vouch for, Mother. But I would not question what you saw with your own eyes."

He asked himself though: *did* he truly believe her? Couldn't that face in the leaves have been anything from a monkey to a projection of a ten-year-old's imagination? After all, the children had all worked themselves into an excited state upon arriving at that mysterious stone in the middle of the forest. They'd had legends of the First Ones on the brain.

He said, "Mother, you mentioned something about the temple you used to go to in town, when you were a child."

"Oh yes, that. Thank you for reminding me, young man. It is most significant. The fire was preceded by the first of my dreams of the Last Ones...

"By that time, I was sixteen, and though you may find it difficult to believe now, I had blossomed into a beautiful young woman. Not so beautiful as my sister Chot, but enough that young men from town began to express interest in me. I even received several marriage proposals, and I begged my father not to accept them. I knew I was destined for another kind of life. One cannot easily explain such a calling to another...though it is the easiest thing in the world to understand for one who has heard it.

"The night of the fire, as I say, I suffered the most horrible dream. I saw a house in which people crept from room to room in the course of unknown tasks, in suspicious silence and wearing strange smiles; at least, when I could make out their faces. Much of the house was deep in shadow, so in hindsight I don't know if all the figures I saw were in fact human.

"Finally, my roving consciousness—which I now understand was my astral self—slipped into a room where a young woman sat in the light of a lantern. Her eyes were glassy, as if she were drunken, or mad, and she was laughing...laughing. Her tunic was unbuttoned, and at her naked breast she held an infant, which appeared to be suckling, though I heard no such sounds.

"The infant, however, was nothing but an inky black mass. It had no features whatsoever. Only a tail, coiled around the woman's wrist.

"I don't believe the First One was actually drinking the woman's milk. Rather, I am certain it was drawing sustenance from feeding on her life force. That is, her very soul.

"As I watched in horror, two human-like eyes opened in the little creature's head—and stared directly into my own.

"I awoke with a scream, and two of my sisters—with whom I shared my bedroom—rushed to my side to comfort me."

Vhek and Jee exchanged solemn looks in unspoken communication.

Mother Xo went on, "I had barely gotten back to sleep when we heard much excitement out in the night. My parents went first to investigate, and we children couldn't resist following them, though we knew we risked being chastised for it.

"Several neighbors were at our door, pounding frantically. They pointed off toward the town, where we saw a red glow in the night sky. The smell of smoke wafted toward our home as well. The neighbors asked my father to go into town with them to help battle the fire. They explained that the temple where we worshipped was being consumed.

"Of course, my father went with them. But despite the efforts of many townspeople, the temple could not be saved, and it burned to the ground.

"Just as the nuns here number twelve, including myself, twelve monks lived at the temple in town, including the abbot. Eight of them ended up perishing…either trapped by the flames, or from smoke inhalation, or days later as a result of their burns. The abbot himself was lost.

"Over the next several years, the four surviving monks helped supervise the construction of this temple you find yourself in now. And perhaps now you will understand why it was built out here in the middle of the river. You see, though it was never proven, it was suspected that the cause of the fire that night was not accidental, but arson.

"Myself, I had no doubts about this at all. You see, while the townspeople still struggled to contain the fire, some reported seeing a woman standing nearby watching the conflagration…and all the while, they said, she stared with crazed eyes, laughing and laughing in a most strange manner."

"Gods!" Vhek said, then he excused himself for his exclamation. "Forgive me, Mother. But…so…what you're suggesting is, the Last Ones intentionally set that fire to burn down the temple and kill its monks?"

"So I believe, young man. So I believe.

"When the new temple was completed, it became the home for the Order of the Ivory Empress. I was one of the first of its twelve nuns, then only a novice of eighteen. The abbess was Mother Uu, then already in her eighties and physically weak, though powerful in spirit. It was my responsibility to tend to her needs, much as dear Sister Kwen tends to me now. Who knows—perhaps one day, Sister Kwen will find herself the abbess of this temple. To my knowledge, she would be the first 'accidental woman' in such a role. Wouldn't that be wonderful, Sister?"

Sister Kwen grinned shyly, bowing her head.

Mother Xo said fondly, "But right now, I'm merely indulging in fancy…"

Jee explained to Vhek, proudly, "Since it was built, this temple has only ever known two abbesses…Mother Uu and Mother Xo."

"At the time," Vhek asked the ancient nun, "did you tell anyone about your dream of the laughing woman?"

"Yes. It was one of the reasons for the decision to build the new temple out in the river, and for a few years this temple was even guarded every night by two of the sisters, carrying lances. But I suppose we grew too lax over time, or too comfortable, and we eventually discontinued the practice. After all, there was never an attack on our temple…until now. And why now? I cannot venture a theory.

"After I related my dream, several women from town were brought before me, in the hopes I might identify the woman I'd seen breastfeeding the infant First One. The men who'd noticed the laughing woman who watched the temple burn were called upon to examine these women as well. One poor creature was mentally disabled, the other addicted to drugs she made from plants she gathered in the forest. Neither was the laughing woman we had witnessed in our different ways. I never dreamed of that person again, specifically…and it was years before I had another dream concerning the Last Ones. Over the years, these dreams were infrequent…until only recently, when they have become increasingly common."

Vhek said, "Mother, if I might suggest, I think it would be a good idea to begin posting two guards outside every night as was done all those years ago. In case, gods forbid, the Last Ones decide to escalate their harassment."

Jee leaned down to her seated brother and asked quietly, "So now you're convinced this desecration was indeed the work of the Last Ones?"

He looked back at her, but didn't reply.

"Mother," Vhek said instead, "I'll start by getting a feel for the town, since I'm not familiar with it. But to be honest, in looking for these Last Ones I don't know where to begin, except to talk to your local police here."

"If it helps you, young man," Mother Xo said, "in these dreams of mine I have sometimes seen the number 777. Sometimes it appears on a wall inside this mysterious house, painted in red…perhaps blood. Other times, it appears outside the house but larger, the letters glowing in the dark—again red."

"I see," Vhek said, and he glanced at his sister again. "777, you say?"

-9-

When they left Mother Xo's quarters, Sister Kwen parted ways with them and Jee led Vhek outside the temple again. The afternoon sun had bloated, slowly sinking earthward with its additional weight. Jee asked, "Have you found yourself a hotel in town?"

"I made arrangements online, but I haven't actually gone there yet."

"I forgot to ask how you came here. Did you rent a taxi, or do you have your own car these days?" Most people in their country made do with motorbikes.

"I have my own car," Vhek replied.

"Fancy."

"You haven't asked me about my family yet."

Jee stopped at a stone railing overlooking the drowsy brown river. Leaning upon it, they watched dragonflies bob just above the surface, like children's toys dangled on strings. In an evasive tone, not looking at him, Jee said, "We haven't been alone yet."

"We're alone now."

She looked up at him suddenly, her smile unexpected and so familiar it hurt. It was as though this was the first moment today in which he had truly recognized his sister's face. "Do you remember when I was little, you'd bring me with you to do some shopping for our parents, and you'd buy me an ice cream stick?"

"Of course," Vhek said. "You always liked coconut best. But sometimes you switched it up with strawberry."

"And you always liked mango...though sometimes you went with durian."

Vhek's own smile felt familiar too. As if he recognized himself finally. "That's right."

"I know a place in town that sells ice cream. Will you buy one for me?"

"Of course," he said, his smile widening.

"Let me just okay it with Sister Fuyen first," Jee said.

"Sister Fuyen?"

"She's the older nun you thought was Mother Xo. She's not the abbess, but she oversees most of the responsibilities here for Mother Xo. She'll become the abbess when Mother Xo passes this year."

"I see. She's really determined to pass this year, isn't she?"

"It's the way she wants it." Jee put a hand on his arm. "Anyway, stay here… I'll be right back. We have to hurry; the ferry will be returning to town soon."

"Will there be another ferry trip before night falls, so you won't get stranded in town?"

"Yes, one more this evening...don't worry. I know its comings and goings by heart."

* * *

Passersby smiled at them, no doubt charmed by the sight of a nun sucking happily at ice cream on a little stick. Hers was coconut. The slender ice cream stick in the hand of the policeman, in his tan officer's uniform, was strawberry pink. The vendor hadn't had either mango or durian. Jee's eyes crinkled mischievously as she reached over to steal Vhek's ice cream too, to have a turn with it for a few slurping sucks before passing it back to him. The best of both worlds.

They sat on a bench in a good-sized park in town. Teenagers in school uniforms walked the paved paths together, some holding hands in a public display of affection their parents would have been too shy to indulge in. Old people sitting on other benches watched these lovers pass, some wistful for their own youth, others bitter with disapproval and no doubt blaming such crude behavior on the influence of foreigners. Elsewhere, on a patch of neatly groomed grass, several middle-aged people went through what looked like a slow-motion version of the martial arts drill Jee and some of the other nuns had demonstrated today in front of the temple.

"You were going to tell me about your family," Jee said, her manner growing a little more serious. She stared off toward some children frolicking on colorful playground equipment under the watchful eyes of their mothers. "How are your boys? They would be eleven and nine now, right?" She had met them at their father's funeral.

"Yes. They're good boys...mostly quiet and studious."

"As their father was. You should bring them to the temple to visit me."

"You're right—I should. I will."

"Please do that. And...your wife?"

"Resentful, mostly, these days. But in her own quiet way. She isn't as vocal with her criticisms anymore, since I found out she had a lover."

"Oh no!"

"Bold of him, risking an affair with the wife of a police lieutenant. Maybe that was part of the thrill."

"What would make your wife do that? You're a good man, Vhek!"

"She says I'm cold. Hard." Vhek had finished his treat and tapped the empty wooden stick in the air. "I showed her boyfriend cold and hard."

"Oh, Vhek... Please tell me you didn't hurt him." *Or worse*, her tone suggested.

"I didn't, but I made him believe I would. I brought him in for questioning, sat him in a little room for a few hours while I interrogated him. I had him in tears a few times without having to lay a finger on him. I guess that made me feel a little less humiliated."

"Oh, I'm so sorry. That's terrible."

"It's the way of men and women. Always has been, always will be."

Fiddling with her own empty stick, in an odd, offhand manner, Jee asked, "So, have you ever taken a lover yourself?"

"No. I wouldn't."

"That's my brother...always so upstanding."

He turned to look at her, to see if she meant this as some kind of secret joke between them. Perhaps a bitter joke. He found her expression unreadable. Her nun's face.

For a moment he was afraid to speak, and wanted to get back the feeling they had shared only a minute ago, but finally he asked, "Do you resent me too?"

"I can't resent you without resenting myself."

"Well, maybe you do resent yourself. I mean...look at the life you lead. Did you become a nun because you heard some great mysterious call, as Mother Xo described, or to run away from...things? From me? From yourself?"

Jee lowered her head, gazing down toward her sandals, the dust that dulled her toenails. He followed her gaze, remembered her cute toes as a child, the pretty pink nails. "It was both. The calling...the running. But I swear, Vhek, I never resented you."

"I hated myself. I always will."

"Stop."

"I think it's the reason I became a policeman. To enforce the law. To see that people are punished for their transgressions. When all the while, it's really me I think should be punished."

Jee waited until two students holding hands strolled past them, giggling and delirious with new love, before saying, "We shouldn't condemn ourselves for it anymore. We were children."

"You were a child!" Vhek hissed. "I was no longer!"

"We were just playing around," Jee whispered, unable to look at his face. Nevertheless, he knew tears were coming to her eyes. "Just wrestling. I sat on you...pinned your arms down...kissed your face to tease you. I was a teenager by then; I should have known better. You were a normal young man...but inexperienced. Still innocent. It wasn't unnatural for you to feel as you did..."

"Don't say that. It was unnatural. It's why it's against the law!"

"We got carried *away*. Our earthly bodies are just machines, with their own purposes. Sometimes they work against us. This is why we should learn to master them, to let our minds and souls guide us and define us instead!" She gasped a little sob.

"I hate to hear you take any blame for it."

"I must!"

"Our parents were right in disapproving of us sharing my bed," Vhek said, his voice hateful, as if he were describing the crimes of someone he had arrested—someone he glared at through the bars of a cell. "I always reassured them it was harmless...that I was just protecting you from your nightmares. And that's all it was…until it wasn't." He wagged his head. "I've always wondered if they suspected, but were too ashamed to ask directly. I wonder if that's why father finally forbade us sharing a bed."

"Please, let's stop talking about this, Vhek."

"Talking about it is too long overdue, Jee!"

"*Enough*. I forgive you. I ask for you to forgive me too, older brother. And then we can finally forgive ourselves."

Vhek flicked his stick away, not caring just then about being a policeman who set a poor example by littering. "You don't need to be forgiven."

"If you're going to be that way, then I'm going to maintain that you don't need to be forgiven either."

"Good," Vhek said, sneering. "Then we can both remain unforgiven. Forever sinful and cursed. Perhaps, one day, to be joined eternally in the Ten Hells. Maybe the demons will marry us there, and sew us together into one wretched body."

"Stop it, will you?" Jee rose from the bench, stooped, and picked up the stick he had thrown to the ground. When she turned toward him, she did indeed have tears in her eyes, but also wore a weird smile on her lips. Partly miserable, partly mischievous. Part nun, part Jee. "If you don't quit talking this way, I'll wrestle you to the ground… Do you understand me? With my martial arts training, there's no way you could win."

She walked away to drop both sticks in a whimsically painted trash can. Vhek stood from the bench, too, and caught up to her. Without holding hands, they walked together along the path, though he recalled holding her hand when taking her into town for ice cream, and then back home again, those many years ago. Sometimes back then they had even linked their fingers like sweethearts.

Still trying to fathom her weird smile, he said, "You've always been strange and unknowable, Jee."

"As are you," she further teased him, looking composed again here in the public eye, but maintaining a bit of that odd smile. "As you say, that's the way of men and women. Always has been, always will be."

-10-

Vhek saw that Jee got safely on the last ferry that would run to the island temple that evening, then returned to his parked car. He finally found his hotel after a half-dozen frustrating wrong turns in the streets at the heart of this town, crammed as they were with narrow buildings painted in pastel colors, most with shops, restaurants, or cafés at ground level.

Before parting ways, he had given Jee the package of gum he'd bought from that sassy little girl after all. He supposed it was because he'd learned she still had a taste for treats.

In his hotel room, with its mostly bare pastel green walls, he turned on the air conditioner mounted near the high ceiling, then opened the container of takeout noodles he'd bought from one of those restaurants facing onto the sidewalk below.

Finished with his humble meal, and having opened a can of white fungus drink from the miniature fridge, he dug out his cigarettes for a smoke. Sitting on the edge of his bed, he turned the cigarette package over and over in his hands. The brand was 777, the numbers printed in metallic gold. Lucky triple seven—the most auspicious of numbers. It was the reason why there was 777 brand beer, 777 brand whiskey and rice wine. That there was a popular coffee shop franchise called 777 Coffee.

Which was why he had felt weary with disappointment when Mother Xo had told him that in her visions of the Last Ones cult, she had seen the number 777 either painted on the wall inside their mysterious dark abode or outside in glowing red. Oh, that was a big help! Lucky triple seven was ubiquitous in their Unnamed Country. It was only understandable that the imagination of a perhaps senile old woman would have added that component to her dreams.

He had almost brought this up to his sister, but ultimately hadn't wanted to be too critical of the woman Jee so obviously revered. He might start to look like a blasphemer himself.

He lit his cigarette, pointed a remote at the wall-mounted TV, and turned it on. He cycled through channels, some crystal clear, some obscured with static, some local, some foreign. He settled on a foreign science fiction/action movie he had seen before, with subtitles in his own language. He watched this for a few minutes before getting up to go out onto the balcony to have a second cigarette. As he pulled the heavy drape aside, he saw the red imprint of a woman's lips on it, where a previous guest had blotted her lipstick.

She'd fucked on that same bed he would lie alone in tonight.

He opened the balcony's doors with their grimy glass panes, stepped out into the sultry night air, an almost liquid thickness after his room's air-conditioned cool.

The street below still buzzed with motorbikes, many with a wife or girlfriend clasped behind the rider, or a sleepy child or two, or loaded with baskets of vegetables. Two pedicabs passed by, each carrying a Western tourist so large they couldn't ride in one pedicab together. He still marveled that these days tourists found their way even to this unnoteworthy town. He supposed they might have come partly to see the beautiful temple of the Order of the Ivory Empress. If so, what, if anything, had these two made of the goddess' empty left hands?

As another bike roared by down there, with a woman in a helmet clinging to the male rider's back, Vhek considered calling his wife to let her know he had arrived here safely and to ask how the boys were. He didn't. The boys would be fine, studying schoolwork or playing video games on the home computer. Though he seriously doubted it, he fantasized that in his absence his wife would see her old lover, or a new lover, every day when his sons were at school. Oddly, this tormenting thought made him aware of the gun holstered on his belt and weirdly aroused at the same time. The latter feeling, when he became more conscious of it, disgusted him. What was wrong with him? With all humans? All of them—in some fashion, and to a greater or lesser degree—shamefully and self-destructively perverse.

What a strange race we are, he thought. And then, a peculiar thought occurred to him.

What if the Last Ones—if that cult truly existed—were right, and the First Ones *were* more pure, more perfect in their simplicity, than human beings? Superior to his flawed and stained, blighted and sinful race, that considered itself the highest order of life? What if the First Ones should have become the masters of the mortal world after all?

*　　*　　*

Pressure on the mattress was what woke him.

The room was so dark that at first Vhek forgot he was in a hotel…forgot he was not in his home city of Haikan. Outside, he heard but one lonely motorbike buzz by in the street.

She climbed up onto the bed slowly, and he almost made out her shape in the gloom. Vhek was confused; he had accompanied her from the park back to the wharf, and hadn't left until he'd watched her board the ferry, along with about a dozen people—most likely locals rather than tourists—keen on attending evening prayers before the temple closed up for the night. Then again, he had waved to her and turned away before the ferry actually pulled out from the wharf, so apparently she'd had a change of heart, and had got off again and walked to his hotel. After all, he had told her where he was staying.

She crawled up beside him, lowered herself at length, her body snugged up against his just as they had used to sleep, except that she was outside the thin quilt, whereas he was under it. Well, at least he had an air conditioner here, and her body wouldn't overheat him as it used to. Vhek was charmed, emotionally moved. And he realized, with her pressed up against him, how lonely he had been in recent years, married though he was. How lonely he had been for *her*. He hadn't wanted to admit it to himself, but here in this near utter blackness, and near utter silence, it seemed safe for the confession.

Often she'd asked him to rub her back; it helped her fall asleep. His mother had rubbed their backs from the time they'd been babies, to make them drowsy. Even years before she took to sleeping in his bed—so that his presence would soothe her, and keep nightmares at bay—she would ask him to rub her back like Mama did; for instance, when they lay on the living room floor watching TV together. Back then, TV reception had been poor and the offerings much more limited, but they had always enjoyed watching repeats of the series that focused on the trickster god Cholukan, with its cavorting lead actor made up in simian prosthetics.

"You shouldn't be here," he said huskily, still groggy, still disoriented. She shouldn't be doing this. But despite his words, he was glad she was here. She was stranded; the ferry wouldn't leave for the island again until the morning. She *had* to stay here with him. And their parents weren't here to fret and disapprove. Their father was dead. His spouse was far removed, in distance and in affection.

She nuzzled her face into his neck. She felt strangely soft, a whispery kind of sensation; he supposed it was her beautiful black hair brushing against his skin.

But then he remembered, as he came a little bit more awake, that she had shaved all her hair off, leaving only that dark stubble. She'd had even more hair than that the first time he ever saw her, when his mother had brought her home from the hospital as a newborn...

He reached over to touch her shoulder. "Jee?" he croaked.

Her eyes opened, and in her otherwise black face they almost seemed to glow. So close to his own eyes, as if she might kiss him in another moment.

Not Jee's eyes.

Vhek cried out, and rolled away from the presence in the other direction. He fell off the bed, but he was beside a little table that he had banged with his forearm, and he remembered he had placed his service handgun there: a foreign-made semiautomatic. His hand clawed for the gun, found it. He sprang upright, pointing the pistol into the darkness, but he wasn't sure which part of the darkness might be the presence. It had either closed those uncanny eyes to hide itself, or turned what passed for its head. Where was the switch for the overhead lights? He couldn't recall.

Then he thought he saw a blackness moving against the blackness, and in his terror he almost fired the gun. He jumped up onto the mattress, then off the other side of the bed. He might not remember where the wall switch was, but he knew where the bathroom was: just off the short hallway that led to the hotel room's door. He found the open bathroom doorway, groped inside, slapped on the overhead light in that room at least.

By the light that spilled from the bathroom into the main room, Vhek saw those heavy drapes with the lipstick stain stirring, as if a breeze had roused them. He darted to the drapes, tore them aside.

He had closed the balcony's doors, even bolted them, after his last cigarette of the night. The presence hadn't escaped this way. Or, at least, a corporeal body could not have escaped this way without the doors being unbolted and opened.

Vhek spun around, gun still extended, and swept his frantic eyes throughout the rest of the hotel room. He saw nothing unusual.

"A dream," he muttered to himself. He had been thinking too much of Jee's dream. Mother Xo's dreams...

Vhek lowered the gun almost reluctantly. He reached up to touch his neck, then looked at his fingertips, as if he expected to see blood on them.

He went barefoot into the bathroom, checked his neck in the mirror, the spot where the presence had nuzzled him. He saw no punctures, no bruises. But would such a creature leave a physical wound as it stole sips of your soul?

"A fucking *dream!*" he snarled out loud, to shut down that line of thought.

But he couldn't shut it down. Not by much. Not here in the deep of night.

He found the wall switch, burned its location into his memory, turned the overhead lights on. He turned on the TV too, lit a cigarette, and sat on the end of the mattress watching a channel that reported on international news. His handgun rested beside him, along with his package of 777 cigarettes.

Only when the rising sun began to tint the horizon a rose-gold hue, out there behind the silhouettes of the town's tightly packed buildings, did Vhek shut off the overheads and stretch out on his bed again to steal a few hours of sleep. He let the TV play on for company, though muted, and kept his handgun within easy reach. For all that was worth.

-11-

Rather than become lost in these unfamiliar warrens of streets again, and then have to find a parking spot along a curb dense with parked motorbikes and food vendors, Vhek simply had the hotel's receptionist summon a taxi for him. In this way he set out for the town's police headquarters.

Stuck to the taxi's dashboard was a little plastic figure of the Ivory Empress, the town's favorite goddess, an off-white color like ivory and with appropriately colored rhinestones in its hands. Vhek made sure none of them were missing. What if all those rhinestones along the lefthand side had been pried off? If only it could be that easy identifying his suspect!

Vhek accepted the young cabbie's business card, in case he ever needed to give him a call, then mounted the steps to the smallish police station and entered. Having folded away his dark glasses, he told the young woman at the front desk, severe in her bright green uniform, that he was a visiting special investigator from Haikan, and asked to see whichever highest-ranking officer was available to talk for a few minutes.

"May I ask what this is in regard to, Lieutenant?" she asked.

"The theft…uh, the desecration at the Order of the Ivory Empress."

"Thank you, sir." The young officer made a call on her desk phone. Vhek heard her relay the information he had given her to someone on the other end. When she hung up, she said, "They're going to see if Captain Khieu is free to speak with you, Lieutenant. Please have a seat."

Having thanked her, Vhek seated himself on a metal bench along one wall. Above him was a large business-style calendar that featured a brightly colored photograph of the temple on its island. He twisted around and looked up to see if any nuns had been caught in the image, one of whom might very well be Jee, but there were none. All inside praying, apparently. At least here, too, the conspicuous statue of the goddess had all of the missing orbs in hand.

He hadn't had a thorough tour of the temple, but suspected items like this calendar and that plastic dashboard ornament could be bought at the temple's gift counter, along with bundles of joss sticks and wads of colorful fake money, the latter meant to be burned and thus sent on to the dead in their afterworld.

A few minutes later, a man in his forties came out from the inner offices and walked toward him. From his uniform's epaulets, Vhek saw he was a sergeant. Vhek snorted, feeling slighted, but he was also grateful not to have to deal with a higher-ranking officer than himself.

The man greeted him, and introduced himself as Sergeant Pan-Koy. Vhek rose from the bench and gave him a polite nod. Vhek repeated the information that the desk officer had relayed, but this time further explained that his sister was one of the nuns at the island temple.

"Ah!" said Pan-Koy. "Your family must be proud of her."

"We are."

Apparently Pan-Koy meant to converse right out here in the lobby rather than invite Vhek back to his office. He smiled and said, "If I might ask, what kinds of investigations do you do there in the big city, Lieutenant?"

"Oh, well, murders, of course..."

"Though even in Haikan, there can't be as many murders as there are in any fair-sized Western city."

"No, you're right in that."

"Do you ever watch the news from over there?"

"I do," Vhek admitted.

"Shameful! The streets are like war zones. If they had firing squads, like we do, they'd see less of that. Less drug traffickers too. Though I imagine you deal with those."

"Yes...rather more drug traffickers than murderers."

"We have few murders here, of course," said Pan-Koy. "The occasional drunk husband putting a machete in his wife's head." He chuckled. Vhek likened the man's crude persona to that of a gangster. They had gangsters, of a sort, in Haikan. Pan-Koy nodded at Vhek's holstered semiautomatic. He himself wore an antiquated-looking revolver. "Ooh!" he said. "May I examine that?"

"I'd rather not take it out," Vhek said. He himself had remained all business, his face stony. "With all respect."

"I see. Well...in any case, how exactly might I be of service to you, sir?"

"Firstly, my sister told me that an officer had come at the temple's request to take a report on the vandalized statue of the Ivory Empress. I was wondering if there had been any progress in that area."

"I don't know, myself, off the top of my head...but I imagine if there had been any developments, the abbess would have been informed."

"Can you find out which officer took the report, and have them contact me?" Vhek gave the sergeant his cell phone number, which the man entered into his own phone.

"Very well…very well."

"Who do you think might be likely to do such a thing?"

Pan-Koy blew out his cheeks. "Ha! I can't imagine *anyone* being likely. Even mischievous teenagers would fear the gods' retribution."

Vhek took on a more confidential tone, as voices tended to reverberate in this lobby. "Are you aware of any cultists here in town, who refer to themselves as the Last Ones?"

The sergeant's leathery, sun-bronzed face crumpled in confusion. "The who?"

"At the temple, I was told of a kind of secret cult that calls itself the Last Ones. An ancient cult that reveres the creatures called the First Ones."

"Ah, the First Ones. I remember my auntie telling me bedtime stories about those, to punish me when I'd been naughty." He laughed, then pretended to shiver. "Brrr! So, what about the First Ones again?"

"Supposedly there's a secretive group that curses the Ivory Empress and the other Jeweled Gods for abandoning the First Ones, and this group calls itself the Last Ones."

"I've never heard of such a group myself, Lieutenant. With all respect to your sister and the rest of them, the Last Ones sound like the stuff of myth, like the First Ones themselves. Not to sound sacrilegious, mind you, but so many of those old fables are, of course, just that: parables meant to entertain and give moral guidance."

"I realize that. Though there is sometimes a kernel of truth in even the most fanciful tale."

"I suppose…I suppose."

"So then you've never heard of the Last Ones yourself, or any other shady type of group here in town?"

"As I say, I haven't. We do have little packs of mischievous youths who fancy themselves gang members, though they're just street rats…nothing like what you must see in Haikan. Or worse yet, the gangs in those hellish Western cities! Imagine having to deal with *that* here!"

"I hope we never do."

Pan-Koy made a pistol-like gesture with both his hands. "Firing squads," he said. "The best deterrent. We must never grow lenient."

"Indeed."

"Ever kill anybody there in Haikan, Lieutenant?" Pan-Koy grinned. "Some out-of-his-mind addict, or drug dealer caught in the act?"

"I haven't."

"Me either. Not in the street anyway, but some years back I was called upon to have my turn in one of those firing squads. I'm sure I hit the target, though our Captain Khieu went over to put one pistol shot into the man's head afterward. We don't hand one man a rifle with a blank cartridge in it, as I hear some countries do to relieve any guilt. I didn't feel guilty at all, but proud to have helped send a fiend to the Ten Hells."

"What crime did this person commit?"

"He murdered his own father during an argument. He tried to claim his father had fallen while drunk, and split his skull on the side of a glass table, but it was determined that he actually struck the old man over the head himself."

Vhek shuddered. He felt that the sergeant was looking at his face too carefully, probingly, watching for his reaction. "I see," he said stiffly. "What were they arguing about?"

"As I recall, the father had insulted his daughter, called her a whore...something to that effect. The son acted impulsively."

"A terrible affair."

"It was. In any case, Lieutenant Vhek, I'll find out who took that report and have them call you as soon as possible. Might I ask, how long do you intend to stay here in our humble town?"

"I have two weeks at my disposal, though I hope to be successful more quickly than that."

"Indeed! I hope we can see that statue restored. Such a blasphemous act. It bothers even me, and I'm not the most devout of men. So, where are you staying? Do you need a recommendation? My cousin runs a nice little hotel by the park."

Vhek told the sergeant he was all set in that regard, and gave his hotel's name.

"I know the place... Good enough!"

"By the way," Vhek said, just to vent a little bitterness. "I had hoped to meet your Captain Khieu. Was he too busy?"

"Perhaps next time," said Sergeant Pan-Koy.

-12-

No good-sized town in his country had only a single temple, so Vhek spent the remainder of the day searching out three others. He summoned back his cab driver to bring him to two of these temples, but walked from the second to the third. In the course of this excursion, he took a break for lunch at a spot in a narrow side alley—where he sat on a red plastic stool befitting a child—that one might generously call an outdoor restaurant. The menu boasted the big vat of broth for the beef noodle soup had never been allowed to run empty, had only ever been added to, and was therefore what his people termed a "hundred-year soup." Were any molecules of the very first batch extant in the bowl that Vhek ate from? He fancied that maybe Mother Xo as a girl had partaken of this same soup he consumed now. When one thought about it, it conjured a strange connection with the past. In any case, the meal was quite good; much better than his complimentary breakfast at the hotel.

The first temple he went to was about the same size as that of the Order of the Ivory Empress, housing a dozen monks rather than nuns, but the building was of a more commonplace design; certainly in a more commonplace location, not being isolated on a manmade island. Its patron god was the Sapphire Emperor, and hence the exterior of the temple was painted a gorgeous blue, with the floor of the shrine hall consisting of blue ceramic tiles, and the altar's backdrop being an impressive mosaic portraying the Sapphire Emperor, primarily in shades of blue.

The monk who met Vhek introduced himself as Brother Bo, and he was friendly to the point of being garrulous. He proudly gave Vhek a tour of the premises, and they conversed as they walked. That is, Brother Bo did most of the conversing.

"Oh no, we've never had any arson here, desecration, anything of the sort… We don't even lock up the temple at night, in case someone in anguish might need to pray to the gods for succor. And yes, our temple was in existence at the time the temple in question was burned down."

Vhek cut in, "Who was the patron god of that temple, by the way? Not the Ivory Empress?"

"It was devoted to no single one of the Ten Jeweled Gods. Not all temples are, as you surely know."

"But was there a statue of the Ivory Empress on the premises?"

"Oh yes, all ten of the gods were represented in the shrine hall, all of them gold-painted statues for an effect of uniformity. Personally, Lieutenant Vhek, I'm not sure I subscribe to the notion that the fire was arson, despite the rumors. The rumors may have covered up for some monk's carelessness with a candle or lantern, or an accident in the kitchen."

"You aren't aware of anyone with a grudge against that temple, or the Order of the Ivory Empress? I've heard that sometimes rivalries can spring up between different temples...bad blood for this or that reason."

"Oh, such shamefulness does occur, sad to say. Like brothers who are devoted to their parents, but hate each other. I really shouldn't indulge in gossip...*but*, some years back, I'm going to say fifty-something, a monk at the Order of the Diamond Emperor here in town fell in love with a nun at the Order of the Opal Empress, and they carried on a secret affair. They were found out, given lashes in the town center, and excommunicated. *Well*, don't you know, it later came to light that the abbot of the Order of the Diamond Emperor himself had been carrying on an affair with the very same nun earlier, and he was jealous that he'd been replaced as her lover by one of his underlings! So the abbot was excommunicated as well...minus the public lashing!"

"Human nature can be an ugly thing," Vhek mumbled. "Our bodies rebel against our minds...our souls."

"Don't be disheartened by the actions of the occasional flawed person of authority," Brother Bo comforted Vhek, as if the policeman had come to him for that purpose. He put an arm around Vhek's shoulders as they strolled.

"Occasional?" Vhek said. "I don't suppose you ever watch the news on TV, do you?"

"I do!" Brother Bo gushed. "But I much prefer historical dramas...the longer the series, the better! Though nothing can beat the series *B-2*, of course. I've seen the whole thing half a dozen times! Those, and game shows. Especially Western game shows. Much less discouraging than the news."

* * *

The temple of the Order of the Diamond Emperor struck Vhek as being on the rundown side, with mold-blackened outer walls in need of being painted over. He supposed its reputation had suffered irreparably those fifty-something years ago when the abbot, and his rival, had been exiled in shame. The temple was now down to six monks, none of them young.

The monk he interviewed had much the same to relate as Brother Bo, though his manner was more guarded, even leery, as if he expected Vhek to bring up that old scandal. No attacks on the temple, no desecrations, no thefts. He'd not heard of anything so shockingly disrespectful in nature occurring at his monastery even before his time as a monk.

Earlier Vhek had asked Brother Bo if he had ever heard about a cult that called itself the Last Ones. He hadn't, and didn't even know what

"Last Ones" might signify until Vhek explained it to him. Likewise with the monk at the Order of the Diamond Emperor.

*   *   *

The Order of the Opal Empress was the town's only other convent. As it was within walking distance of the Order of the Diamond Emperor, Vhek could imagine how the two monks and one captivating nun had easily managed to arrange their rendezvous.

This temple, too, had seen better days, the tiered levels of its roof missing more than a few tiles, the paint on its window shutters flaking badly. However, its interior offered some striking effects, such as the altar's backdrop: a representation of the Opal Empress done in a mosaic formed from bits of iridescent nacre, obtained from freshwater mussels, to engender an opalescent effect. The statue of the Opal Empress outside was impressive as well, though one might feel the goddess was portrayed in too sensualized a manner. Vhek idly wondered if the artist had had some mortal woman he loved, or longed for, in mind as he sculpted her.

The abbess, Mother Nal-Lan, met with Vhek herself. Only half as old as the ancient Mother Xo, she knew the venerable abbess well enough and spoke of her fondly.

Seated with Vhek in a little office room where she conducted any business-type matters, Mother Nal-Lan listened to what Vhek had to say, then chimed in with the others: there'd been no attacks, no attempts at arson, no vandalism or thefts. The worst they might encounter was, for example, a drunken man who had wandered into the shrine hall at night and fallen asleep on the floor while praying to the Opal Empress for forgiveness for being a drunk.

"If there is indeed such a group as these Last Ones," Mother Nal-Lan said, perplexed, "why would they have waited all this time, from the burning of the old temple until now, to get up to mischief again?"

"Who can say?" Vhek said, seated before her desk. "If they do exist, they must have their reasons, which we—not being part of their cult—can't fathom. Maybe they take action based on some celestial occurrence; an eclipse, the passing of a comet, the alignment of certain planets or stars. This may be a significant year for them."

"Hm. It is the year that Mother Xo has become one hundred and twenty-three," Mother Nal-Lan said.

"That's right. She said it was a significant year for her. And so maybe for these people as well, being enemies of the Ivory Empress. They may be like two faces of one coin."

"But it's all too bizarre, Lieutenant. Oh, I don't mean to suggest I doubt Mother Xo and her visions, but...to think such a group could have existed all these years, all but unknown, under our very noses?"

"So you'd never heard rumors of them before?"

"Not I. One seldom even hears people tell the tale of the First Ones, let alone the suggestion that there are devotees of the First Ones. Though, I suppose, my sisters at Mother Xo's order would be more conscious of that fable, bearing in mind the First Ones' connection to their creator, the Ivory Empress." The abbess frowned then, her forehead rumpling in thought. "Huh!" she said.

"What is it, Mother?"

"I just remembered something...an experience that was related to me about a month ago, I'd say, by a woman who came here and begged me to say a protective prayer over her daughter."

"Why was that?"

"Well, as best I'm able, I'll tell you her experience, just as she described it to me...

"This woman said she was awakened one night by her baby crying in its crib in the room next to hers. Her child was about six months old then. This woman got up to go to the little girl, expecting that she had wet herself or had a bad dream. When she stepped into the room, however, she saw a figure leaning over her daughter's crib, perhaps reaching inside. It looked to her as if someone was trying to lift the child out...or at least was staring at the child very closely.

"So the mother cried out, and lunged at the figure. In that moment, she didn't even think to turn on the overhead light; she thought only of grasping this intruder and pulling it away from her daughter.

"As she tried to put her arms around the figure, though, she said it spun away from the crib...and its body slipped right through her arms. The woman told me it was an uncanny sensation, like trying to hold onto a human figure made of water. 'Water that wasn't wet,' was how she described it.

"The woman believed it was a ghost she saw, and I couldn't help but feel the same, because I have seen ghosts with my own eyes. But, our discussion just now made me recall the last detail of this woman's story. She said the dark figure plunged right into the corner of the room, as if there were an opening there. Just then, her husband appeared in the bedroom's doorway, having heard his wife cry out, and he flicked on the switch to the overhead light.

"As the light came on, the woman told me that both she *and* her husband saw what looked like a thick black snake disappearing into the corner of the room. It was only an instant, she said, but she had the impression that this snake-like shape was the phantom's tail."

Vhek's throat clicked as he swallowed. Another story to add to the rest...to his own. He managed to get out, "Was the child...was she all right?"

"Well, she was alive, but the woman told me she was very weak and pale for several days afterward. The child still looked feeble when I saw her and prayed over her, though I urged the woman to take her to a doctor, in case she was ill with something."

"Mother...do you believe the thing she and her husband saw could have been a First One? Not a creature of fable, but some actual type of entity we really know nothing about?"

Mother Nal-Lan held Vhek's gaze with the utmost solemnity. "I don't know, Lieutenant. I don't know."

-13-

Vhek thought he should fill his sister in on what he had, or hadn't, learned that day, so once the taxi driver had returned him to his hotel, he took his own car down to the wharf by the river, so as to catch the ferry's last trip to the island temple for that day. He found a good number of people already filing aboard, as with yesterday at this time—townspeople who wished to attend evening prayers.

Vhek rushed to fall in with the others, ducked his head under the ferry's awning, and in glancing about for a good spot to sit—preferably on a bench that he could have to himself—saw a woman twisted around in her seat watching him. She smiled politely when their eyes met and gestured for him to come join her. He recognized her as Sister Fuyen, the nun in her fifties whom he had originally assumed to be the convent's abbess.

Vhek squeezed down the aisle between the rows of benches to settle beside the woman. "Thank you, Sister" he said. "Were you in town on errands today?"

"Yes, Lieutenant. As Mother Xo is too old to deal with the day-to-day matters of running our temple herself, I'm often called upon to go into town on this or that errand. I send the younger sisters if it's just about going for food supplies, but there are more business-type matters that demand my personal attention. It may sound crude to put it that way, but..."

"Oh, I understand."

The nun held up a carboard box she had set on the bench on the other side of her. "More figurines of the Ivory Empress, to provide to worshippers in return for a small donation."

"I see," Vhek said. That was a nice way to describe the temple's selling of souvenirs.

"We are very fortunate that a company in town, that molds a variety of plastic products, manufactures these at no cost to us. The factory owner is a very devout man."

"That's good of him."

"What of your own errands in town today, Lieutenant?"

He told her of his visits to the three temples; that none of them had experienced similar harassment. "I can only assume," he concluded, "that the individual or individuals involved in the desecration have a singular grudge against your temple, or to be more precise, the Ivory Empress herself."

Sister Fuyen nodded as she listened to him, smiling primly in what he thought was an indulgent manner. When he had finished, the nun said, "As you can imagine, Lieutenant, I have nothing but reverence for Mother Xo. However—and I confide this in you solely because of your position as an investigator, and to be helpful in that regard—I wouldn't give too much credence to what she says about the First Ones, and a secret group that devotes itself to them to the extent that they've made themselves enemies of our beloved Ivory Empress. You've met Mother Xo. You're aware of her profound age. She hasn't left the temple in decades. She dwells as much in her dreams as she does the reality of the waking world. I fear that in her mind, the First Ones of old, old stories that precede even the adventures of Cholukan have taken on a literalness they were never meant to convey. They were parables then, and are the mere shadows of folk tales now."

"So one would expect to believe," Vhek said.

Sister Fuyen narrowed her eyes slightly in their fleshy pouches, as if she felt he had worded this statement oddly. "How could one truly believe otherwise?"

The ferry continued chugging along, and a familiar atmosphere of incense announced their approach to the little island. Along with the drifting scent drifted a recording over loudspeakers: droning chants punctuated by deep gongs. A prelude to the evening prayers.

For a minute, Vhek looked down into the river and watched its water slop against the boat's flank, then turned back to Sister Fuyen and said, "So you'll take on the mantle of abbess when Mother Xo passes? This year, if she's to be believed?"

"Yes. It is quite an honor and responsibility."

"Have you been with this temple since your youth then?" He thought of young Sister Kwen, and Mother Xo's fond wish that she would be the one to hold the position of abbess one day.

"Actually, no. I came here only three years ago—from a temple in Haikan, in fact. Perhaps you're familiar with it? The Bhen Jop Temple, on Lido Street? It faces onto the river there."

"Is it next door to a café?"

"It is! A great banyan tree stands between the two buildings."

"Okay, yes. I've been to the café...not to the temple. It's tended by both monks and nuns, is it not?"

"Yes."

"Does that ever make for...ah, pardon my asking...awkward situations?"

"No," Sister Fuyen said, a bit tersely. "The dormitories for monks and nuns are on opposite sides of the main building, and are locked at night, with a trusted guard watching over the grounds."

Vhek wanted to tease her that even trusted guards could be bought, or seduced themselves, but didn't want to appear any more disrespectful or unprofessional than he might already seem for asking. Instead, he asked, "That temple isn't devoted to any patron god or goddess, is it?"

"Correct."

"So what brought you out here to the Order of the Ivory Empress, Sister?"

"The passing of the previous assistant to Mother Xo...Sister Shong. She wasn't an elderly woman, being only about my age, but she suffered a fatal heart attack."

"Oh, that's terrible."

"Mercifully, though, she apparently died in her sleep."

"A stressful dream, perhaps," Vhek said.

"Excuse me?" Sister Fuyen said.

"Just speculating. I'm sorry; I never know when to stop. It's my mindset. In any case, congratulations on your reassignment...and your soon-to-be important promotion."

"Promotion is a funny way of putting it."

"Again, my apologies. I'm a secular man."

The ferry, with its buffer of rubber tires, bumped up against the temple island's dock, and a young nun darted forward to help tie the craft off. Its passengers disembarked, Vhek lending a supporting arm to Sister Fuyen…though, having watched her in martial arts practice, he figured she was as least as tough as he was. He assumed she accepted his assistance only to meet politeness with politeness.

The sun was just at the horizon, the heat-hazed air gone a pumpkin color, shading toward violet. The worshippers, familiar with the routine, were already heading for the shrine hall, bending to remove their shoes or sandals on the broad marble step just outside.

"Oh—have you come to see your sister?" Sister Fuyen asked Vhek, as they too strolled toward the shrine hall.

"If that's all right. It won't be a problem if I distract her from evening prayers? If not, I can wait until they're over."

"Better not to wait for that, or you may miss the ferry back to town. It's fine, Lieutenant…I'll go fetch her for you."

"Sister! Sister Fuyen!" cried a voice behind them.

Vhek and Sister Fuyen turned to see a nun running toward them, breathless. It was the young sister who had secured the ferry at the dock. Her duty there finished, she had rushed after them to catch up. "What is it?" Sister Fuyen said, sounding a bit irritated for having been startled, or perhaps feeling that this excited display was unseemly.

The nun panted, "Behind the temple…please go see…there is some animal there that was trying to come onto the island."

"Some animal? What animal?"

"We don't know!"

Without waiting to see how Sister Fuyen would respond to this, Vhek was already moving at a trot, circling around to the right of the temple and its adjacent wings. He saw a number of worshippers, preparing to enter the shrine hall, look over at him in curiosity, and he heard quick footsteps following after him—undoubtedly, those of Sister Fuyen and the young nun.

As he came around to the rear of the temple, near a low stone wall at the island's edge—where it dropped away into the listless flow of the river—he spotted his sister Jee with several other nuns, plus a Western couple and their young child.

A split second after taking all this in, he spotted the animal in question.

Along with Jee, Vhek recognized Sister Kwen, the "accidental woman," former bar girl turned nun. Kwen especially caught his eye because in her fists she held a lance with a long flexible handle and a nasty-looking spearhead. The set of her face made it clear she was ready to lunge forward and thrust with the lance should the animal draw any closer to the island.

The Western couple were youngish, and the father had picked up his son, whom Vhek guessed to be about two years old, and held him protectively against his chest. Father and mother turned to Vhek, his policeman's uniform drawing their attention, looking both alarmed and angry, as if upset with him personally that tourists should encounter anything distressing on their vacation to the Unnamed Country.

Jee saw her brother hurrying toward them, and turned to him with wide eyes to gush, "Vhek, do you see that thing?"

"I see it."

Sister Fuyen fell in beside Vhek and listened, too, as Jee explained the situation.

"These tourists here were taking pictures, and their son wandered off only a few feet, throwing pebbles at the water, and that was when his parents looked and saw that thing moving toward him through the water. When they scooped him up, it stopped advancing...but it's still there!"

Vhek moved closer to the stone wall to look down at the creature.

With the nearness of evening, and in the deep shadow of the temple upon the murky water, the creature was little more than a black humped shape standing several feet above the river's surface, somehow stationary in the heavy flow. Behind the shape, a loop of tail curved out of the water and entered it again. The only discernible features were two staring eyes in the front of its face like those of an owl. These eyes caught the glow of the setting sun and shone redly.

"It's a snake," Sister Fuyen said. "A python. They can grow over twenty feet."

"I don't think that's a snake," Vhek said.

"Of course it is! What else would it be? You're seeing it head-on. The rest of it is under the surface."

"It won't stop staring at our son!" the Western father said, and Vhek understood enough of these words to gather their meaning, given the context of the situation. "Look at it! It still wants him!"

"I think I can hit it with the spear if I throw it!" Kwen said, shifting the lance over her shoulder and bouncing it there to get the right feel for it.

"You will not," Sister Fuyen said. "Put that down, silly boy!"

Even as Kwen suggested throwing her lance, Vhek had drawn his handgun out of its holster. He glanced over at the Western couple, and jerked his head to indicate they should back away with their son.

The couple did so, and the mother reached quickly to cover her son's ears with her palms, but when Sister Fuyen saw the pistol in Vhek's hand her eyes all but bulged from their sockets.

"Stop! Don't you dare, Lieutenant… Don't you dare shoot a gun here on these holy grounds!"

"I'm sorry, Sister," Vhek said, lowering the semiautomatic before he could thumb off its safety. "I just don't want that thing harming anybody here."

"It won't! It's just curious! Give it a moment and it will go away, I'm certain." Sister Fuyen shoved Kwen toward the tourists. "Get them away from here…take them inside the temple. If it doesn't see the boy anymore, it will undoubtedly leave."

"It's not a python, Vhek, is it?" Jee said, coming close to him.

"I don't think so," he replied in a low voice. He hadn't yet returned the gun to the holster at his hip.

Looking stricken by Sister Fuyen's words, Kwen with her lance ushered the tourists away, and just as the older nun had predicted, almost immediately the black shape with its fiery eyes began to sink straight down into the water. Its eyes lingered at the surface, staring now directly at Vhek—or so it seemed to him—just as the sun lingered like a balloon caught in the silhouetted trees beyond the river. The eyes reflected there in the water a few moments, then finally submerged, and were extinguished.

"There," Sister Fuyen said, heaving a sigh. "Just as I said. I saw a snake that large before, years ago, swimming down the river alongside the Bhen Jop Temple. They're frightening, I realize."

One of the other nuns who had witnessed the scene said in a shaky voice, "I know, Sister. In the village where I grew up, a giant snake was found swallowing a pig whole, before the owner of the pig killed the thing with a machete!"

"That Kwen," Sister Fuyen said, turning to Vhek and wagging her head. "Making a big drama, with his spear. He should have taken that couple away from here immediately, instead of making them more agitated. I swear, when Mother Xo passes I'm going to send that silly boy away. He has no business here at a convent."

Jee and Vhek looked at each other. Vhek knew his sister well enough to tell she wanted to speak up in Sister Kwen's defense—both for having fetched that lance and for being here at the Order of the Ivory Empress like any other nun—but she held her tongue.

"You too, Jee," Sister Fuyen said. "Why didn't you get those white people away from here right away?"

"I'm sorry, Sister," Jee stammered. "We were just so stunned... We didn't know how to react to the situation. That thing..."

"You should have let me shoot it," said Vhek, watching Sister Fuyen's face. He said it as much to gauge her reaction as to draw the woman's anger away from his sister. "That thing could come back here."

Sister Fuyen glared at him. "I doubt that. It was a freak incident. Those creatures aren't as common around here as carp, you know. As I told you...I won't have firearms being used on these sacred grounds, Lieutenant."

"Well, sorry to say, my duties must come first. If I see people endangered, it's my responsibility to protect them. If I should be here and that creature or another like it appears, I'll do what I have to do."

"Perhaps, then," Sister Fuyen said, "it's a mistake having you here at our temple to investigate the desecration, Lieutenant. Perhaps you should go home to Haikan, and leave it to our capable local law enforcement to investigate the matter."

"Sister Fuyen, with all respect, a crime has been committed...and now being aware of that crime, I must do as my job dictates. The nature of that crime is a blasphemy so severe that it transcends this one temple—isn't that so? It's a crime against the Ivory Empress herself, I would say. Don't you, devoted to the goddess as you are, see it that way yourself?"

"You don't need to tell me how seriously to take this matter!" Sister Fuyen all but spat. "Nevertheless, I find your attitude arrogant and disrespectful. It appears your sister was wrong in asking Mother Xo's permission to summon you here, and I think now I should have a word with your captain back in Haikan..."

"You'll do no such thing, Sister Fuyen," hissed a faint, creaking, and yet somehow forceful voice behind them.

They all looked to see Mother Xo standing between them and the rear face of the temple, where the door to the dormitory in which the abbess had her quarters stood open. For just one moment, Vhek thought she was a ghost standing there, with her gray complexion, her robe hanging off a scarecrow's body of lashed-together sticks. Several of the nuns, including Jee, cried out sharply. Vhek almost did himself.

Jee darted to the cadaverous woman's side and put an arm around her to hold her upright. "Mother!" was all she could exclaim.

"Mother Xo!" Sister Fuyen said. "What are you doing? You could fall!"

"Sister Fuyen," Mother Xo said, ignoring their protests, "I have every confidence in Lieutenant Vhek. He is here to help us. He *will* help us. I saw it in my dream just now. He stood under the glow of the triple seven, and saw its red light reflected in the eyes of the First Ones, where they sought to blend into the darkness. They are coming...coming for revenge, for being slighted. We can't see them with our insiders' eyes as well as Lieutenant Vhek can with his outsider's perspective..."

"Get her inside!" Sister Fuyen snapped to the other nuns.

"I'll help," Vhek said, going to the abbess' other side and putting his own arm around her.

"Would you carry her, Vhek?" Jee implored.

"Of course. Forgive me, Mother," he said, as he gently bent and collected the woman into his arms.

"Be careful not to trip," Jee said, gathering up Mother Xo's trailing robe and tucking it around her.

"She might have fallen and struck her head!" Vhek heard one of the nuns say to another, moved to tears at the abbess' unexpected appearance. "I haven't seen her step outside the temple in all the years I've been here!"

"Careful, careful," Sister Fuyen said to Vhek as he turned toward that open door, carrying the abbess against his chest. She seemed to weigh less than the sapphire robe bundled around her. "Watch her head going through!"

Jee placed a hand atop Mother Xo's head as Vhek passed through the threshold, lest it bump into the doorframe, but Vhek had never carried even his own infant sons with such a level of caution.

Inside, they went down the hallway into the abbess's quarters, where Vhek slowly, so slowly, lowered her down onto her bed and the pillows that allowed her to sit partly upright. He looked into her face as he did this, and she was smiling at him, her white-glazed eyes seemingly aglow with an inner radiance, her visage both hideously skeletal and blissfully child-like at the same time.

"Thank you, young man," she told him. "Thank you. No soul is unstained, remember that. We are flawed children, all of us, even myself. The Ivory Empress understands this. She understands *you*. She pities you...but she still loves you."

Unnerved by these words, Vhek said nothing as he slipped his arms out from under the abbess and straightened. Behind him, he heard the tearful nun whisper to Sister Fuyen, "She's delirious, Sister. I fear her time of passing is close!"

"Shh," Sister Fuyen said. When Vhek looked over at her, she was watching him and said, "Thank you, Lieutenant."

"Whatever I can do to help. Should I summon a doctor?"

"No doctor," Mother Xo rasped, shutting her lids in the shadowed pools of her sockets. "No doctors, please. I will return to sleep now." Her words trailed off dreamily. It almost seemed as though she had been sleepwalking this whole time.

"Thank you again for your help," Sister Fuyen said to Vhek, drawing him aside by the elbow. "I spoke too rashly to you. We will honor the Mother's wishes, of course. For now, though, you should prepare to leave before the ferry departs without you for the night."

Vhek nodded, gave a grunt of assent. He glanced once more at Mother Xo, who already appeared asleep, then looked to his sister Jee.

"I'll see you out, Vhek," Jee said. She ushered him out of the room and toward that rear doorway, rather than cutting through the shrine hall where the evening prayers were underway.

They walked together to the dock, where the ferry bobbed in the brown soup, the pilot slumped down in his chair obliviously with the blue light of his cell phone on his face. Above them, the sky was a deepening blue. The chants and gongs emanating from the temple were no longer a recording over speakers, but the actual voices of several of the nuns leading the prayer service, with one of them striking a gong to produce a low, resonating hum to punctuate the monotonous chanting. Even from here, it seemed to vibrate inside Vhek's chest.

"I think she's feverish," Jee fretted, glancing back toward the temple. "She must be failing. How she found the strength to come outside, though…"

"We have a few minutes before the service concludes, yeah?" Vhek said. "Good…because I have some things to tell you."

Jee looked up at him. "That you've found the Last Ones?" she asked.

"No," he said. "That the First Ones are no myth. You saw one just now yourself. And you saw one as a child." He drew in a breath, and finally admitted to her after all these years, "I understand, now, that I saw one as a boy too."

"Vhek!"

"And last night, one of them came for me again…"

Vhek again stayed up late into the night with his hotel room's lights on and the TV running without sound as he lay back on the bed looking through his cell phone, conducting searches on the First Ones. Though many of his countrymen were online these days, and had a presence on social media and video sharing sites, all that he found were a couple mentions of the First Ones in the context of his country's most obscure folklore. Not one account of a sighting such as he and his sister had experienced...let alone an event like the one from earlier that evening, witnessed by so many.

At some point he dozed off while reading, but since his cell phone's charger cable was connected it didn't run out of power, and it was the phone's ring that awoke him. He struggled with disorientation for a moment until he realized he was here and not in his own home, and by the strip of light blazing into his room between the closed drapes he determined it was well into the morning. He snatched up the phone, and as he stared at its screen it took him another moment of disorientation to recognize the number as belonging to Sergeant Pan-Koy of this town's police force.

He took the call. "Vhek."

"Lieutenant," came the sergeant's voice, sounding rather more serious than Vhek remembered it, "have you heard what happened in town last night, by any chance?"

"In town? No, I haven't." Unless the sergeant had heard about the incident at the temple, with the so-called python? But then, he would know Vhek had been there himself. "What happened?"

"Last night, three of our townspeople died. One of them was a child of only eleven months, found dead in his crib. Of course, that kind of mysterious death is not uncommon with infants, sad to say, and it might not otherwise seem unusual...but also, two adults passed away, also in their sleep, also without any known cause as of yet. Of course, they were both elderly and not in good health. One was a man of seventy-two, the other a woman of eighty-one."

"Well, that is a lot to have happened in one night, I suppose, for a town of moderate size. Certainly it's tragic...especially about the baby. But why do you feel this matter concerns me?"

Vhek dreaded the answer, because he felt he already knew why Pan-Koy had called him about this. Sleeves of gooseflesh covered his arms.

Pan-Koy said, "You had asked me about a cult devoted to the First Ones, remember? Well, something odd was seen last night by a grandson of the old woman who died. He heard her moaning in her sleep, and went into her room to look in on her...as I said, she was known to be in poor health. Well, the boy said he saw an animal crouched on the old woman's chest, pinning her to the bed."

"An animal..."

"The boy said it was a black leopard. He couldn't see it well in the dark, but said it had a long tail. When the boy came in the room, this animal leapt off his granny and the boy didn't see where it got to after that. His screaming brought his father into the room—the old woman's son—but with the lights on there was no sign of any black leopard. However, the son discovered his mother lying there dead with her eyes and mouth wide open. As if in shock."

"I see."

"*Do* you see? What I'm getting at is, the thing the boy swears he saw reminds me of the First Ones, the way my auntie described them in those spooky old stories she told me as a boy."

Vhek said nothing. As the sergeant had related the account, Vhek had pictured the event with awful cinematic vividness.

"Lieutenant?" Pan-Koy said. "I'm sorry...I know how I sound."

"No, don't feel self-conscious. I'm glad you let me know about this, Sergeant. In fact, I'd like to question this boy myself. The families of the other two victims as well, if you can arrange it."

"Well, I would just want to clear that with Captain Khieu first...you being a visiting officer and all."

"Fine, but there's no need for you to get into why, exactly, I want to speak with these people. I'll tell your captain myself."

"Good. I don't want him to think I'm going mad."

*   *   *

In the meantime, because Vhek didn't want to just sit in his hotel room feeling restless and impotent, he called that taxi driver again, who by now he knew by name: Twanh. While he waited outside the hotel on the sidewalk smoking a 777 brand cigarette, Vhek wondered where he would tell Twanh to take him once he got there. To go see Jee, and tell her about the three fatalities last night? She didn't have a cell phone herself by which to call her, and he didn't want to call the temple's office and most likely have to speak with Sister Fuyen now that there had been friction between them. Anyway, he embraced any reason to see his sister in person now that they had been reunited, so to speak.

Ultimately, though, when he climbed into the back of the cab he instructed young Twanh to drive him to the police station. He hadn't heard back yet from Sergeant Pan-Koy, but hoped the captain would have the decency this time to meet with him in person.

However, when they were about a third of the way to the police station, Pan-Koy finally called him back, with frustrating news.

"I'm sorry, Lieutenant… I spoke with Captain Khieu, and he said he doesn't want you speaking with the families of these three dead people."

"Why not?" Vhek snapped.

"He just says our office can handle the matter on our own."

"So, one of these stupid rivalries, is it? Like when government investigators try to help solve some local crime, and it becomes a biggest dick contest?"

"Sir, I can't really respond to that, can I?"

Vhek sighed irritably. "Well, thanks for trying, Sergeant. I just wonder, now, what your town is supposed to do to prevent more of these incidents from occurring."

From the second or two of silence on the other end, Vhek could tell the possibility of such a thing knocked Pan-Koy back a step. "Do you think there'll be more of these deaths, Lieutenant?"

"Who can say? But why wouldn't there be? Especially among the weak and vulnerable, like the elderly and children. Until…until I don't know. Until maybe these spirits get stronger and can suck the life out of healthier people as well." Vhek didn't know if he believed in what he was saying, but he had needed to voice the possibility. To keep even his wildest fears to himself would make him feel complicit should things unfold as he described.

"But even if we told Captain Khieu about what we suspect, what could he do? Even if he believed us and took it to our province's government committee? How do you safeguard against…you know, against what you're suggesting? Do we tell families to rotate guard duty over their sleeping family members?"

"I have no answers, Sergeant. Right now, only a lot of confusion and helplessness."

"Maybe all we can really do is ask all the monks and nuns in our town to pray hard to the gods for their protection."

"Perhaps," Vhek muttered, looking out the window at townspeople innocently going about their day, unaware that tonight when they darkened their bedrooms they might be in serious danger. "I don't know what to do at the moment, except go to see my sister at the convent…and maybe speak with the abbess again, if I can."

"That may be a good idea, like I said. Lieutenant…I think by the end of this, you and I are going to become more religious than we previously have been in our lives."

"I don't know about that. Less skeptical, anyway."

Vhek ended his call with Pan-Koy.

"Twanh," Vhek said, leaning forward a little to address the cabbie. "Change of plan. Turn us around and take me to the ferry. I'm going out to the Order of the Ivory Empress."

-16-

In order to reroute his cab away from their previous destination and toward the ferry wharf, Twanh turned his cab down a side street Vhek hadn't been on before.

Seething with frustration, feeling like he was canned up inside this car, canned up inside his own skin, Vhek stared out the window at the buildings sliding past. Much like the buildings he'd seen in other streets in this town…in other streets of any town of the Unnamed Country. Street-level businesses with apartments above them. With their doorless faces open to the street: a beauty salon, a shop that sold heavy wooden furniture lacquered a deep red, a little café, a bar with a sign advertising 777 beer, a shop that sold motorbike tires wrapped in brightly colored plastic sleeves…

"Stop," Vhek ordered Twanh.

"Sir?"

"Stop the car… Pull over here!"

Rather than pull over to the curb, Twanh was so startled by Vhek's tone that he laid on the brake in the middle of the road to let him out. A motorbike that had been riding too close to the back of the car was forced to come to a stop with barely an inch of room between the vehicles. The bike beeped its horn angrily, and the rider started shouting curses at the cab, whipping off his helmet as if he might use it as a weapon. However, when Vhek emerged from the cab in his tan investigator's uniform and stood there glaring from behind his dark shades, the rider put his helmet back on, gave an awkward little salute as if he were a fellow policeman, walked his bike back away from the cab, and rejoined the narrow street's traffic…which was being forced to maneuver around the stopped cab, though with Vhek standing conspicuously beside it there were no further complaints.

Leaning out his window, Twanh asked, "Should I stay here waiting for you, sir?"

"Not if you're going to continue running the meter. I may only be a minute for all I know, but if you have somewhere else to be, then go on. I'll call you when I need you, and if you're busy I'll get a ride from someone else."

"Nowhere else I need to be at the moment, sir. I'll pull over just ahead and wait here unless I get another call."

Vhek crossed the street at an angle, motorbikes smoothly veering around him. He walked back toward that bar with the sign advertising 777 brand beer hanging outside.

Had this been a bar in Haikan, particularly in an area that attracted tourists from abroad, such an advertisement might be in neon, but this sign was rust-spotted metal, the 777 painted bright red against a white background. The lamp positioned directly above it was shut off now in the day, but at night must make the reflective sign seem to glow. As for the name of the bar, it was less showily printed in red letters on a grubby yellow awning that ran above the bar's entrance. This looked like a dark cave in the building's face of yellow-painted plaster, the brick beneath showing through in crumbling areas, with a single window covered by decorative metal bars inset above the awning. The gaping entrance's security shutters were folded back to either side for the day, and even as he approached Vhek couldn't see anything inside but deep gloom.

He came to the entrance and paused, removed his sunglasses, and finally got some sense of the interior. He mounted a single concrete step and slipped inside.

A lone man with a plastic-looking pompadour sat at the end of the bar, speaking with the bartender. When Vhek entered, their low conversation ended and both men looked over at him. Likewise, a man sitting at a corner table with a much younger woman—who from her suggestive attire Vhek took to be a bar girl—looked up at Vhek as well. The bar girl tittered nervously, as if caught at something red-handed.

Vhek went to the bar, took a seat a couple stools over from the customer with the pompadour. The bartender slid over to Vhek, who was tapping a 777 cigarette from its pack.

"Help you, sir?" asked the bartender.

"Hmm…what to drink?" Vhek said, stroking his neat goatee. He gestured with his as-yet unlit cigarette at another sign for 777 brand beer, this one smaller than the one outside, hanging over the shelves of bottles behind the bartender. "Guess I'll have one of those."

"Yes, sir." As the bartender produced a cold bottle, popped its cap, and poured it into a glass, he casually asked, "Are you visiting our little town, sir? I've not seen you before."

"Yes, I'm a visitor," Vhek said. He accepted his glass, into which the bartender had added a good-sized chunk of ice to keep it cold in this tropical heat. Vhek took a sip and sighed approvingly. "Ah—that's what I needed."

"What is it about our town that attracts you, sir?" asked the patron seated at the end of the bar, as he took a sip from his own glass of beer.

"Well, I'm here to investigate the desecration of the statue of the Ivory Empress, out at the island temple," Vhek said. "You must have heard about that."

"Sorry, sir," said the man with the pompadour. "I haven't."

"Yes," said the bartender, "a terrible thing. Kids these days."

Behind Vhek, in the corner, the bar girl tittered again.

"I guess so," Vhek said, taking another small sip of his beer. "Say, do you have a restroom I could use?"

Vhek noticed the bartender narrowed his eyes a fraction and hesitated fully a second before answering. "Yes, sir. It's in the hallway upstairs."

Vhek swiveled on his stool to take in a curtained doorway at the back of the room. Sliding off the stool, he thanked the bartender and walked toward the doorway. He glanced at the bar girl and her john at their table as he passed. Both watched him go by, both of them smiling. Past the doorway's curtain, years of cigarette smoke interwoven in its fabric, he found a metal staircase.

The bathroom was at the head of the stairs, in a short murky hallway with a floor of worn-through linoleum tiles. There were three other doors, all closed: two in the opposite wall and one at the end of the hall. Bedrooms for the building's owners, Vhek supposed. He shut himself in the filthy bathroom and found he really did need to relieve himself. Nothing looked unusual in the bathroom, and he wondered: *Why would it?* What exactly did he expect to see up here?

What had compelled him to enter this building was what he'd already seen outside, repeated over the bar. 777…777…

Returning to the hallway, he paused to consider the three closed doors. Should he open them, peek inside? He decided against it…for now, at least. However, he was very much conscious of the increased deepness of his heartbeat. There was an energy here…an energy that had perhaps even drawn his eye as he'd passed the place in the taxi. Or was the energy simply his own, generated by a mind that was spinning its wheels?

Just as he was starting for the stairs to return to the bar, the door at the end of the short hallway opened a fraction with a secretive creak. Startled, Vhek looked that way and saw part of a face peeking out at him, and one glassily shining eye.

"Sorry," Vhek said. He jabbed a thumb over his shoulder. "Just using the restroom."

The face looked rumpled; perhaps the flesh of an elderly person, but much too white. A woman who used some damn bleaching cream to make her face look lighter like a Westerner's? His wife used those potions, and ended up looking like a shiny ceramic doll (while from neck to feet the rest of her remained brown), though Vhek had told her the stuff might be linked to cancer. Or could this woman be wearing thick white pancake? Perhaps, because her lips appeared to be painted a red as bright as her skin was white.

The face—what he saw of it—unsettled Vhek. That loose skin, and the contrasting darkness around the one staring eye (was that makeup also; too much eye shadow?). Vhek had a disturbing thought. That this might be the laughing woman, now elderly, whom Mother Xo had seen in a dream suckling an infant First One. Who was, in turn, the laughing mad woman spotted at the time of that temple's burning...who might even have been responsible, herself, for setting the deadly fire...

But no, the idea was irrational. Mother Xo, now almost a century and a quarter old, had been a teenager then. The laughing woman would now be even older than the abbess. Impossible. That strange woman was long dead.

Vhek stammered—even as he began speaking, not sure what he meant to say—hoping to coax this person into opening the door wider and talking with him, but the uncanny white face pulled back and the door clicked shut.

Vhek hesitated, contemplating whether to knock on the door. He didn't. Instead, uneasy and frowning, he went to the stairs and descended.

When he had pushed past that long-unwashed curtain, Vhek saw that a new customer had seated himself at the bar in his absence. On the stool right next to Vhek's own. This man was also a policeman, in a green uniform with the epaulets of a captain. He had laid his visored cap on the bar, and openly watched Vhek as he approached his stool and reseated himself.

"You must be our visiting investigator, Lieutenant Vhek from Haikan," said the police captain.

"You must be Captain Khieu," said Vhek. "It's nice to finally meet you."

"Indeed. Sorry I couldn't do so earlier…a captain has many duties to attend to."

"Yes…your Sergeant Pan-Koy informed me that you were too busy to see me just now."

"Ah, not quite true," said Captain Khieu, lifting an upward-pointing finger to stop Vhek. "I didn't say I was too busy to see you today…I simply told Pan-Koy to relate that I'd prefer you didn't question the families of those three people who passed away in their sleep last night. No disrespect is intended, but I don't see the point in troubling those traumatized families any more than is necessary, given that their situations are sadly commonplace."

"Commonplace? Do you think so, Captain?"

"Think so? Why wouldn't I? Two elderly people in poor health, plus a child who passed from Sudden Infant Death Syndrome. Tragic, but hardly unusual."

"Have you not been told about the stranger aspects of these cases, Captain?"

Khieu drew in a long inhalation through his nostrils, seeming to assess Vhek for a moment before replying. "Was it that blabbering sergeant of mine who told you that nonsense? I need to have a stern word with him. Really, Lieutenant…a grandson claiming a black leopard was crouched upon one of the dead, and yet she was found not to have a scratch on her?"

"Suppose it was some other creature that the boy mistook for a black leopard?"

"Another creature such as…?"

Vhek didn't know if he should go on. But, being convinced that more lives were at stake, he couldn't afford to put pride before responsibility. "Are you familiar with stories of the First Ones, Captain? The proto-humans said to be designed by the Ivory Empress, and released to our world prematurely?"

The bar girl giggled so loudly this time that her companion shushed her harshly.

"Lieutenant…really?" Khieu said, looking ready to chuckle himself. "Please tell me you don't believe in such nonsense. My goodness. Forgive me saying this, but it's definitely a good thing that I stopped you from questioning these people's families."

"Maybe you should listen to all I have to tell you. Some of it can be backed up by nuns who witnessed an event with me at the convent...not to mention some tourists who—"

Khieu held up a hand again to cut Vhek off, his expression having become less amicable. "Enough, Lieutenant...that's quite enough now. I must insist you not come to my town and stir up the citizens with old folktales. We have real day-to-day concerns to deal with here."

It was like talking with Sister Fuyen all over again, Vhek thought. Very much like that. "Have you never heard of a cult that worships these supposedly imaginary First Ones? Because rumor has it that such a cult exists in this very town."

"I have heard no such thing...the very thought of it is ridiculous. It's so illogical—especially coming from a man of your position, a man who works in our nation's capital, no less—that the very suggestion makes me angry."

"Well, I hope you're right, Captain, for the sake of any such cult," Vhek said, watching the older man's face carefully. "There are a lot of devout citizens in this town, I have no doubt...devoted to the Ivory Empress and the other nine Jeweled Gods. If such a cult did exist, and your devout citizens knew who such cult members were, I'm sure they'd string them up in the street before you and your officers even got there to see to the matter yourselves."

By the end of what Vhek said, he noted that Khieu was all but gritting his teeth. "I suggest you leave my town as soon as you can, Lieutenant, before I put in a call to your superior to report your irresponsible behavior. You seem intent on stirring up trouble here, and I won't have it. So what if a few colored balls were stolen from the island temple? They have no practical value. They've probably already been smashed or tossed away into the forest by the teenagers who stole them as a prank."

"You dismiss those orbs, part of an important holy monument, as nothing but 'colored balls'? Isn't that a rather blasphemous attitude, Captain?"

"Lieutenant Vhek... I'm afraid I'm going to have to ask you to finish your beer and leave this establishment. You're disturbing the customers."

Vhek produced some bills, paid for his beer, but left the glass mug untouched except for the two sips he'd taken before leaving to use the toilet. He didn't trust that it had sat there unprotected in his absence. "By the way, Captain, I'm just curious...who told you I was in this bar, after I'd gone upstairs to use the restroom?"

"What are you on about now, Lieutenant?" the captain growled. "No one called me...I come to this place all the time!"

"Do you now, Captain?" Vhek said. "Do you now?" Then he turned away and walked toward the open front of the bar, which framed the contrasting brightness of the street outside.

He saw that Twanh's cab still waited for him a little way up, across the street, and went to it. As he reached for the left rear door handle, he felt his attention pulled back to the bar...a strange sensation, as when Twanh had driven past the place just a short while ago.

In that lone window above the bar's awning, Vhek saw a white floating blob that hadn't been there when he'd first approached the bar.

He knew it was that same too-white face with the too-red lips and sagging flesh, spying on him as he departed.

-17-

Vhek drove to the wharf in his own car, thankfully without taking any wrong turns in his distracted state, and found Jee waiting for him there as she'd promised. Wanting to speak with his sister freely about what he'd found and what he suspected, he had taken the chance of evoking Sister Fuyen's displeasure by calling the temple to see if Jee could come out to join him for lunch. Fortunately, it was a younger nun who'd answered the phone and fetched Jee for him.

Vhek waited in his car for Jee to finish speaking with an older woman who held the nun's hands and appeared to be smiling with tearful gratitude. An injured soul, but weren't all souls thus? After Jee had listened to her and spoken some words of comfort, the woman pushed a little money into Jee's hand; a donation to the temple. Jee politely made a gesture of refusing it, but the woman insisted. Finally Jee spotted Vhek idling there and came to enter the car, immediately filling it with the scent of incense.

"Does Sister Fuyen know you're escaping for a while to see me?"

"I haven't seen her today...she may already have come to town herself. This is the day of the week she normally does so."

"To do business?"

"No, not on this day. Lately, about once a week she looks in on a sick old aunt. Does some cleaning and errands for her, cooks enough food to last her through the week. Sister Fuyen usually doesn't come back to the temple until the last ferry."

"Oh?"

"Occasionally she's missed the ferry and had to sleep over her aunt's place, then return in the morning."

"Huh. I see. Well…that's kind of her, to help out her aunt." Vhek started easing his car into the swarms of motorbikes. "Have you ever met this sick old aunt yourself?"

"No, I haven't."

Vhek was silent for a few seconds. Sometimes, deeper parts of his mind worked busily behind a curtain, in hiding from his conscious mind, but he had learned to entrust them to their duties. "Are you hungry?"

"I could eat."

"So we can speak in private, we should get something to go and take it to my hotel."

Jee agreed, and this they did: picked up a few submarine sandwiches packed with cold cuts, pâté, and pickled vegetables, with a side order of rice paper rolls filled with cold noodles and shrimp. Iced coffees too.

He sat on the edge of the hotel bed, she on the room's single chair. Vhek watched Jee spread their humble feast out on a little side table, gazing at the exposed back of her neck where it swept down from her stubble-shaded skull. That spot looked both familiar and alien to him. In their youth, he would have had to pull her long hair away from her nape to expose it. He remembered kissing her there, and squirmed with desire and self-loathing. He tore his eyes away.

He sipped his iced coffee, thick with sweetened condensed milk, and when he set the plastic cup aside he saw that Jee had turned and was trying to read his face.

"So tell me what's going on," she said. "Have you found out something about those people who died last night?" He had told her that much over the phone. Out on their island, the nuns hadn't heard.

Restless, Vhek got to his feet and paced a little. He hesitated before speaking, and when he began his back was to her. "You know I've never been much of a believer, Jee, but I've heard it said that nothing will drive a doubter to belief in the gods quicker than the workings of demons."

"Are you becoming a believer at last, Vhek?"

"Do you hope so?"

"Of course I do. I've never told you how many times I've prayed that you would. Maybe…oh, it's foolish. But maybe you were summoned here for that very reason. To save your soul."

Vhek turned to look at her. "So you feel I'm damned if I don't redeem myself? Admit it, Jee. You aren't wrong for that thinking…it's the basis of your belief. You know exactly which of the Ten Hells sinners must go to for the specific crimes they commit. I can never remember how that works, though I've seen the damned punished in their hells in amusement park attractions. Tell me, which Hell would I go to for what I've done to you, and haven't atoned for in the eyes of the Ten Jeweled Gods?"

"Vhek, the gods see *all* of you. Your flaws…yes, your sins…*my* sins…but they see our goodness too."

"But I haven't officially repented, as you have. Do you know, Jee? I'll confess it to you. Not just that time our father accused you of being another man's child, and I held a knife to his throat. Other times too…even after you answered your calling, and I was there to listen to his ugly drunken words alone. What I'm saying is, I wanted to kill him…to *truly* kill him. To smash his skull in with a heavy pot, or even beat him to death with my own fists. I could see these scenarios play out in my mind. Later, these feelings would fill me with self disgust and guilt, to the point that when he finally died, I was irrationally afraid that people might suspect I had done away with him somehow. As if they could see through me…see all those hateful, poisonous thoughts."

"Father wasn't an easy man to live with much of the time. He had his own pain too. But he did love us, Vhek—you *and* me."

"Yes, which makes my terrible feelings all the more sinful. In the olden days, in Emperor Tho's time, you know what they did to someone who murdered their own parent? They punished them with the death by a thousand wounds, because it was considered the gravest of sins. And here I am, someone who considered—who ached to commit—such a sin. Add that to what I did to you. Add that to remaining married to a woman who doesn't love me, keeping her from her lover out of pride and jealous spite. How could I ever make myself clean before your gods?"

"Vhek…"

"What, Jee? What can you say? You see, before I came here I felt I had done wrong…done bad things…but I never thought of my behavior in the sense of *sin*. But *now*…now that I feel the beginnings of belief, belief such as you have…"

"You worry for your soul."

He looked at her miserably.

Jee stood up, stepped closer to him. "The gods can be harsh, but they understand human beings are weak. Very weak. Just as parents still love their children when they behave poorly. I'm *happy*, Vhek…happy that you are finally opening yourself to the actual existence and love of the gods."

Vhek's eyes were filling. He couldn't remember when he had last shed tears as an adult. Had he ever?

Jee went to him, hugged him and held him against her body. They had not even embraced at their father's funeral. Her bare neck was near to his lips, but he didn't press them to her flesh. He put his arms around her clumsily, awkwardly rubbed her back.

Jee laughed a little, her breath against his own neck. "Ha. Do you remember, Vhek, when I would ask you to rub my back as a child? You would sit watching TV, trying to enjoy some cartoon, and this needy brat would lay her head in your lap and expect you to rub her back like a spoiled little empress."

Vhek chuckled. "I remember, Jee. I remember well."

"Vhek," she said gently, close to his ear, "when you return home…cut your wife free. I don't say this out of any jealousy—you know that. Stay in your sons' lives, but set her free. Set yourself free from your anger."

Vhek didn't know how to respond, but just then his cell phone buzzed. Jee stepped back from him, and he looked to see who was calling. Pan-Koy.

"Vhek," he answered.

"Hello, Lieutenant. Did you hear? But how would you hear? My bastard captain has suspended me for two weeks without pay. Can you believe that? All because I talked to you about those three deaths we had last night."

"I'm sorry, Sergeant."

"Don't blame yourself. He's a bastard—I'm not afraid to say it. He berated me right in front of everyone at the office. Spitting mad! I can't imagine why he's so upset about it, except that he probably feels intimidated by having an investigator from Haikan in our little town."

"I think there may be another reason why he's so upset about this topic, Sergeant. Something having to do with an experience I had today, right after we spoke on the phone before."

"Oh?"

Vhek looked at Jee meaningfully, to let her know he was going to be explaining to the both of them at once. And then, he proceeded.

In the course of it, he even told them how he had felt strangely drawn to the bar…suggested that maybe even the driver Twanh, with his plastic figurine of the Ivory Empress stuck to his dashboard as if to guide him, had unconsciously been impelled to take the investigator down that particular side street.

Vhek said, "I might not otherwise have read so much into the bar having a big red 777 outside, and a smaller one inside, as Mother Xo saw in her dream. After all, come on, 777 is everywhere you look in our country. But when I came downstairs and saw Captain Khieu, of all people, sitting there..."

"Do you think the bartender or one of the customers called him?" asked Pan-Koy. "Or do you truly believe, like he said, that he goes in there often?"

"Do you know him to frequent that bar?"

"No, but I've never even really noticed it before, to tell you the truth. But, Lieutenant...what you're suggesting...it's mostly just based on hunches."

"Intuition. Revelation. Call it what you will. Maybe it's just my investigator's instinct. But I feel that today, I stumbled upon the place Mother Xo dreamed of—the place where the Last Ones gather. And Captain Khieu's presence there, and his animosity toward me..."

Pan-Koy said it for him: "You think Khieu is one of them."

Vhek and Jee looked into each other's eyes grimly.

-18-

Vhek and Jee sat in the back of Twanh's taxi with the engine turned off, a little ways up from the bar on that side street as before. Twanh had been exceedingly polite to Jee, and insisted he would not take money for his assistance on this excursion; he had only asked Jee to bless the figurine of the Ivory Empress stuck to his dashboard. She had touched it, closed her eyes, and moved her lips in silent prayer.

Now Jee leaned across Vhek's body to look toward the bar. Vhek had told Twanh not to park directly opposite the place, lest they be too noticeable, but they could still get a good look at it from this angle. The open front with its metal shutters folded back, the old yellow awning with the bar's name in red letters, the large metal sign bearing the lucky triple seven in red.

"It doesn't look like much," Jee said.

"Exactly. Nondescript. Perfect."

"For what, sir?" Twanh asked.

"Just play your game, Twanh," Vhek told him, and the young driver returned to the game on his cell phone.

"Vhek," said Jee, with a touch of urgency coming into her voice.

"What?"

"That face in the window…"

She sat back into her own seat so she wouldn't be obstructing her brother's view.

There it was again. That grotesque white face, floating at the window over the awning. "That's her," said Vhek. "The old woman who peeked out at me in the hallway."

Vhek got out his cell phone and activated its camera feature, but when he zoomed in on the second-floor window, the white face had already withdrawn back into the darkness behind those decorative metal bars.

"Probably just the bar owner's mother," Twanh said, not looking up from his game.

"Quiet," Vhek told him.

Vhek watched two young men on one motorbike, perhaps taking a late lunch break from some job site, dismount at the curb and go on inside the bar jauntily.

"What are you thinking now, Vhek?" his sister asked him.

"I want to come back at night and watch for what time they close. And then watch them some more."

"Do you want me to pick you up for that, sir?" Twanh spoke up.

"No. I think this time I can find the place on my own." He turned in his seat to face Jee. "I wish you had your own phone so I could tell you developments directly. Let me buy you one right now, Jee."

"No, Vhek… If I got caught with it, I could be disciplined, and then we might not be able to see each other again at all."

"You could mute the ringer…just leave the phone on vibration…"

"No, Vhek. I'm sorry."

He sighed. Returned to watching the bar. "I wonder if I should contact my office at this point. Tell my captain what I've found thus far. The thing is…I'm afraid I've only found enough to make him believe I've lost my mind. Just enough for him to order me to leave here and not come back."

"You see, Vhek," the blue-robed nun told him. "We both have to be careful what we do."

"For now," he repeated, "I'll just have to see what this place looks like at night."

"If you see something suspicious and act on your own, it could be very dangerous," said Jee.

"I won't do anything foolish. I just want to gather some real evidence…something to prove this cult really does exist. Then, with that in hand, I can call in more people from Haikan to come flush these cultists out and deal with them. But things are much more urgent now. Before, it was only about recovering some stolen property. Now, it could be about preventing more deaths."

Twanh looked up wide-eyed at his rearview mirror, but this time he was too intimidated by the policeman's ominous tone to ask him what he meant by that statement.

*   *   *

Vhek rode with Jee on the ferry back to the island temple. He hoped they wouldn't find Sister Fuyen had already returned from caring for her sick aunt, only to discover that Jee had gone into town without her permission and thus become angered. However, Sister Kwen came to meet them straightaway and let them know Sister Fuyen hadn't returned yet. The young nun's face was tight with concern.

"Mother Xo hasn't been well today," she reported. "She hasn't really woken up, not even to eat a little soup. She's sweating and has a bit of fever, so I've been putting cool compresses on her head. We've been saying payers for her too. Sister…I'm afraid her time might be coming soon."

"Oh no," Jee said. "Have you been able to reach Sister Fuyen about it?"

"No. Her aunt doesn't have a phone. Or if she does, no one knows its number." Kwen shifted closer to Jee and lowered her voice. "Mother Xo talks in her sleep sometimes. I know it's just the fever, but it frightens me. Sometimes she talks in a small voice like a little girl."

"What does she say?" asked Vhek.

"I'm not sure…it's hard to hear…but I've heard her say the name 'Chot' a few times. Chot was her older sister, the one who passed away at only twenty-three."

"The one who went into the forest with her boyfriend that day," said Vhek. "The day Mother Xo saw the First One hiding in the tree."

Kwen said, "Perhaps the spirit of Mother Xo's sister has come to guide her to the Ten Heavens."

The three of them were silent for a moment.

Then, Jee took her brother by the hand. "Come to the altar, Vhek," she said. "You and I will pray for Mother Xo together. We won't beg the gods to spare her life, because Mother Xo doesn't want her life spared past this year. We will only pray that if it is time for them to take her, that her passage to the Ten Heavens is a straight one, and that the gods take her into their arms with all their love."

Vhek hesitated. Him, pray at an altar? But it was only a moment's hesitation, and he squeezed Jee's hand. "Very well."

"Also," Jee added, "I will pray for your safety tonight."

*   *   *

They waited until a last couple tourists left the shrine hall to tour the grounds elsewhere before the next arrival of the ferry. Within the hall, the lighting was subdued, with an equally subdued loop of chants and gongs issuing from speakers, and the burnt-paper scent of incense was enough to fill the lungs. A shy novice who tended a glass counter off to one side of the hall sold Vhek a thin bundle of joss sticks. Vhek also slipped some folded bills of money into a donation box before he and Jee approached the altar side by side, like a bride and groom. Jee had left her sandals, and Vhek his shoes with his socks tucked in them, just outside the shrine hall entrance.

The only one of the Ten Jeweled Gods present at the altar was the Ivory Empress, but this representation of her was much smaller than the desecrated statue outside, which was nine-feet-tall even in a seated position. This version was the size of a seated mortal person, and thickly coated with metallic gold paint so as to appear solid gold, unlike the larger white stone figure. The deity's elevated platform was flanked by two huge vases, and positioned to either side of her was a large flower arrangement and a bowl of fresh fruit. Two smaller flower arrangements, two smaller bowls of fruit, and two tall candles were positioned more to the fore. Between these flanking items rested a large bronze urn filled with sand, and spiked into this was a forest of joss sticks burned down to their bright pink ends.

As with the greater statue, nine of this figure's graceful arms were extended out from her slender body. In each upturned palm was affixed a spherical glass candle holder, individually colored to represent the nine other Jeweled Gods. In the five arms radiating from the goddess' right side were globes that corresponded to the colors of the Jade Emperor, the Diamond Emperor, the Sapphire Emperor, the Topaz Emperor, and the Garnet Emperor. The candles flickering inside them caused the variously colored globes to glow softly, beautifully.

None of the glass spheres were missing from the palms of the four arms extended from the statue's left side. There was a deep red candle holder for the Ruby Empress, and holders with subtler shades for the Pearl Empress, the Opal Empress, and the Quartz Empress. And, of course, the Ivory Empress' tenth arm was folded up between her breasts with her fingers bladed under her chin to indicate herself. Her face was lovely—serenity personified—with eyes closed, full lips sealed and faintly smiling.

Jee took two incense sticks from the package Vhek had bought and lit them from one of the tall flanking candles. She waved the flames out and handed the sticks with their glowing, smoking tips to her brother. She then lit two sticks for herself. Watching her, Vhek wondered why his people so often burned two sticks, and not one or three. More symmetry, he supposed.

He knew the motions at least. Duplicating his sister's actions, he bowed his head, closed his eyes, and held the joss sticks up by his forehead in both hands.

It wasn't until he did this that he realized he wasn't just going through the motions after all. No…especially not since the conversation he had had with Jee earlier that day in his hotel room.

With his eyes closed, he realized he was immediately, actually, praying.

He prayed for Mother Xo; that her passage to the Ten Heavens would be a straight one, and that the gods would take her into their arms with all their love.

And he implored the Ten Jeweled Gods to forgive him, and especially his sister, for their sins.

He asked for the gods to watch over his sons, now and throughout their lives. He promised to release his wife from their loveless marriage. For the first time since the man's death, he prayed for his father's soul to find peace. He considered asking the gods to watch over him tonight when he went out to spy on that little bar, but he felt too self-conscious to do so. Let Jee do the praying for that.

In return for all this, he vowed to the Ivory Empress that he would right the wrongs that had been done to her by her ungrateful human children. And by her first race of children too.

-19-

While Vhek knew some of the fancy clubs in Haikan that catered to foreign tourists might stay open to 2 or even 3 in the morning, generally throughout the Unnamed Country bars closed at 12 or as early as 11. It was presently just before 10, and Vhek's car was parked a bit farther up from the bar and across the street, just as Twanh had done hours earlier.

In fact, Vhek received a text from Twanh just then, from inside the bar. He had decided to rent Twanh's services tonight after all…though he had ordered the young man to come on his motorbike instead of in his conspicuous taxi, especially since that old woman upstairs had no doubt seen it before. The bike was parked just ahead of Vhek's car.

The update texted from Twanh's cell phone in their native language read: *I've ordered a beer. Don't worry, I'll drink it slowly. Besides the bartender there is one man at the bar, and a couple at one table.*

Vhek texted back: *Is the woman a youngish bar girl type? Laughs too much?*

The reply came. *Yes. She laughed when I came in and looked at her. Annoying.*

Vhek: *No policeman in there?*

Twanh: *No, sir. Just those I've mentioned.*

Vhek: *Innocently ask the bartender what time they close. Again, be careful not to let anyone see you're texting. Make them think you're playing a game.*

Jee leaned forward from the backseat, where she'd been trying to keep low and in shadow. She whispered, "So, is that Captain Khieu in there?"

"No," Vhek said. "Maybe he's not coming. Maybe nothing will happen tonight."

"Mother Xo thinks something will," Sister Kwen reiterated. She was slumped down in the backseat too.

*　*　*

A few hours earlier, Vhek had been called by Jee using the temple's office phone. When Vhek had confirmed for his sister that he was presently at his hotel, she'd said, "Don't go anywhere…I'm sending a messenger to your room soon."

"A messenger?"

"Don't ask right now. Vhek, Sister Fuyen hasn't come back yet…no word from her. Just to let you know."

"And Mother Xo? How is she?"

"Still mostly sleeping, still feverish, but she woke up briefly and spoke to Kwen."

"What did she say?"

"The messenger will tell you."

Actually, it was two messengers who eventually came knocking at Vhek's hotel room door: Jee and Kwen. After letting the two nuns in, he said, "It's late...how are you supposed to get back to the temple tonight?"

"We can't," Jee answered. "We took the last ferry back to town. Sister Fuyen got stuck in town tonight herself, right? If she finds out later we couldn't return to the temple too, I'll tell her the same thing happened to me and Sister Kwen. We came to visit you and ended up staying too late."

"But *why* did you come?"

"To accompany you tonight when you investigate the bar. You said that Sergeant Pan-Koy refused to go with you."

It was true. Vhek had called Pan-Koy, trusting him enough to reveal his plan. He'd asked the local policeman to come with him as a witness, and as back up, in case Vhek determined the cult was present and should be moved in on.

"Oh gods, Lieutenant," Pan-Koy had said at that time. Vhek could visualize his wincing face. "I can't believe you're asking me this."

"Why not?" Vhek said. "I thought you agreed with me that your town faces a serious threat. And you haven't tried to convince me that your captain isn't a part of it all."

"But...but for me to oppose him! And he outranks you too!"

"I'm sure my office will stand behind me, if only I have some solid proof of the cult's existence. They'll protect both of us!"

"Lieutenant," Pan-Koy said, with pain in his voice, "I just can't...I *can't*. I'm suspended for two weeks anyway, remember? Yes, we do need more proof, like you say, but we need it before we can act."

"We won't get that proof *until* we act!" Vhek all but shouted.

"Lieutenant...I'm sorry."

"Damn you, Pan-Koy," Vhek said, and then hung up.

In his hotel room, exasperated, Vhek said to Jee, "Even if I do decide to move in on the cult tonight, I can't have you two endanger yourselves."

"And we can't have *you* doing anything like that without extra eyes and hands."

"But if Mother Xo is so ill now," Vhek countered, frustrated, looking to Kwen, "do you really think it's a good idea to leave her side?"

"I wouldn't think that, normally, not at all," Kwen replied. "My place, first and foremost, is at Mother Xo's side. However, when she was briefly conscious, she told me her sister Chot had visited her in her dreams. Mother Xo didn't tell me what her sister said to her, but she told me I needed to go with you tonight, wherever it was you were going. Sister Jee too. She *ordered* us to accompany you. How could either of us disobey her? If Sister Fuyen does take us to task for leaving the temple tonight, I will make Mother Xo's wishes known to her."

Vhek gave up arguing after that. No wonder Jee hadn't told him her plan over the phone, had spoken of a "messenger" and surprised him here. It was too late to turn them away now. And anyway, who was he to oppose these two determined nuns...and their abbess besides?

* * *

Twenty minutes passed, and no other customers entered or left the overlooked little bar on this overlooked little side street. Vhek found himself watching the window over the entrance more closely than the entrance itself...expecting to see that white face appear again, to peer out at the night. It didn't. All the while, he wondered: now that it was dark, and many townspeople would already be sleeping—mainly children and the elderly—would the ghostly remnant of a First One be abroad, seeking to feast on their life energy? Maybe even more than one such primeval ghost? Gaining in strength even as their victims dangerously weakened? And him just sitting here helplessly...

Then, a new text came from Twanh.

Have to leave. Policeman came downstairs. Said they need to close early.

All right, Vhek texted back to him. His heartbeat was like a deer startled into flight by a gunshot. He didn't want to write more and detain the cabbie at his cell phone.

Vhek twisted around in his seat to show the text to the two nuns. "Khieu is in there. He was in there all along. Upstairs."

"Oh!" Jee said. "And what was he doing up there?"

"I'm going to find that out."

The three watched avidly as Twanh soon emerged from the bar's murky interior. Vhek felt strangely relieved that he had escaped safely. Twanh made a good job of crossing the street and straddling his parked motorbike without looking toward Vhek's car, let alone speaking to him. Only when he started the bike up and swung it around to leave did he finally make eye contact with Vhek through the car windshield. They nodded at each other, and then Twanh was buzzing away.

"All right," Vhek said aloud, just as he had said in his text. "First, we wait for those other three customers to leave, if they're closing early as Khieu says."

"*If* they leave," Kwen said.

"Exactly."

Even as Vhek said this, out from the bar stepped a man who took hold of one of the security shutters and began to unfold it with a noisy rattle.

"Is that the bartender?" Jee asked.

"No," Vhek said. "That looks like the man who was sitting with the bar girl when I went in there. The customers *aren't* leaving."

With that, Vhek had his door open and was ducking out of the car. He bolted into the street.

Jee and Kwen didn't even need to look at each other; they were instantly following Vhek's lead, slipping out either side of his vehicle.

The customer had at this point dragged the one shutter to the center of the entrance, and was moving to take hold of the other. However, hearing Vhek running toward him, he looked up with an expression of surprise. The man appeared to hesitate for a moment as he decided how to respond, and then quickly began to unfold the second shutter. He meant to lock Vhek outside.

Cutting across the street at an angle, Vhek increased his speed, hoping to reach the man first, tempted to yell for him to stop but afraid that would alert the bar's occupants. It was then that Vhek saw another man running toward the bar from the opposite direction, and this man had a pistol in his hand.

Vhek's heart jolted. Was this a cultist come to oppose him, to keep him from getting inside? As he ran, he reached for his own gun…even as he finally realized this man with the gun was Sergeant Pan-Koy in street clothes.

For a terrible moment, Vhek thought that Pan-Koy had betrayed him. And here he had trusted the man, told him everything! He'd probably alerted Captain Khieu…

Pan-Koy had already been walking toward the bar before breaking into a run, and so he reached the man at the shutters first, pointing his old revolver at the customer's startled face.

"Don't you lock that gate or I'll blow your teeth out the back of your head," Pan-Koy hissed, loud enough to command but not so loud as to be heard inside. He kept his gun trained on the man until Vhek, huffing, reached them. On Vhek's heels came the two nuns, who'd run silently like gusts of night wind.

"I thought you didn't want to come," Vhek whispered to Pan-Koy, catching his breath.

"I still don't," said the policeman, "but here I am."

Vhek drew aside the shutter the customer was holding onto, seized the man by the shirt, and yanked him onto the sidewalk, away from the entrance lest anyone inside look out and see them. "Who's inside?" he demanded, pulling his own handgun and jamming its muzzle under the man's jaw. "And don't think of calling out and warning anybody."

"Just the bartender," the customer babbled, wisely keeping his own voice lowered. "He's counting the till, so he asked me to lock up for him!"

"Liar," Vhek said. "I know for a fact there are at least five other people in there." He checked them off in his mind even as he said it: *Khieu...the bartender...the man with the pompadour...the bar girl...the old woman upstairs.*

"I don't know anything about that!" the customer protested. "Look, I was just about to go home!"

To Pan-Koy, Vhek said, "Handcuff this one. Is your car nearby?"

"Just back there a ways," the sergeant replied, jerking his head behind him. "I'll lock him in, then come back. I just hope we're doing the right thing, Lieutenant."

"Take him," Vhek told him. "I'll go on inside before they get nervous that this one hasn't come back yet."

Pan-Koy looked dubious about Vhek going in before he could return, but then he saw the two nuns standing behind Vhek each held a curved, single-edged sword in one fist that he hadn't seen them withdraw from beneath their sapphire robes.

"Okay," Pan-Koy said, and then he roughly took the customer by the arm and spun him around. Holstering his revolver, he set about shackling the man's hands behind his back.

Vhek looked to the two nuns and gave them a crisp nod.

-20-

In most bars and restaurants of the Unnamed Country, one could find a miniature altar somewhere in the room, either on the floor against a wall or up on a shelf. Within a little enclosure of lacquered wood, traditionally, or these days of plastic—lit by artificial candles with red bulbs—would be sheltered a figure of the Ruby Empress, most people's favorite of the Ten Jeweled Gods, or even a figure of that goddess's pet, Cholukan, her spy in the mortal realm. In a bar, there might be offerings of unopened beer cans along with the usual fruit.

It was only now on his second time entering this bar that Vhek realized there was no altar.

He shot his gaze to left and right, his handgun echoing that movement, quickly ascertaining that no one else was down here in the bar itself. The lights were as dim as ever, but somehow without occupants the room seemed even darker.

Vhek stole toward the curtained doorway at the back of the room, training his gun on it. Behind him, the two nuns parted to either side in case anyone came flying out at them, but when Vhek ripped the curtain back, no one was behind it…only the narrow metal staircase to the second floor. He looked over at his sister, then turned and began creeping upward.

At the top of the stairs: the little hallway with four doors. Two in the lefthand wall, closed as before. One door in the righthand wall, and though it was also closed, he knew this to be the bathroom. Then, the door at the end of the hall through which that old woman had peeked. He understood from its orientation that it was the room with the lone window that faced upon the street.

Behind the door to that front room, Vhek thought he heard several low, muffled voices, and he definitely smelled incense burning. He moved forward stealthily, reaching out his free hand…

Just as his fingertips brushed the doorknob, the toilet flushed in the bathroom and its door swung open. Vhek whirled around to see the man with the pompadour who had been sitting at the bar the last time he'd come here. Only, that time the man hadn't been entirely naked, as he was now. He had two human-like eyes tattooed on his chest, one above each nipple, but no other facial features were inked there.

"Hey!" the man said.

Kwen, closest to the bathroom door, cocked back her sword arm to threaten the man to remain quiet, but he was fast and lunged forward, catching Kwen's arm in both hands to prevent her sword from descending.

"Help! Help!" the man cried out.

Then Jee was in motion. She swung her right leg up in a powerful arc and kicked the man square in the throat, causing him to release Kwen's arm and fall backward into the bathroom. Kwen was immediately standing over him, holding the point of her sword ready to jab into his belly if he tried to get up—but the man was too busy choking, unable to draw breath, his eyes bulging in a face going red.

The voices in the front room changed in tone. There was no time to waste. Vhek turned the knob, finding the door unlocked, and barged into the room gun-first.

The dimly lit front room was devoid of furnishings or features, apart from a side table and that one barred window, and the five people who stood within it were also naked, though only four of them were human.

One of these people was Captain Khieu, and upon seeing Vhek burst into the room he darted toward the table where bundles of clothing were folded, as if ashamed of his nakedness. Also on the table was what looked like the flayed face of an old woman, with too-white skin and too-red lips, white hair attached to its scalp. It was a rubber mask, such as a child might wear during the Festival for the Dead, when each year families honored the spirits of their ancestors.

Vhek barely noticed Khieu, or the naked bartender and the two naked women—the bar girl young and attractive, the other one in her fifties. His eyes were locked on a figure that stood in the center of the room within a white circle painted on the old linoleum tiles. At five points of the circle rested a brass bowl, each filled with sand, into which two incense sticks had been inserted. In four of the bowls, atop the sand, rested an orb. A red orb that represented the Ruby Empress...an opaque white orb that represented the Pearl Empress...an iridescent orb for the Opal Empress...and a clear, smoky orb for the Quartz Empress. But each orb had been shattered more or less into equal halves, as if struck with a hammer and chisel.

In the fifth bowl, atop the sand rested the head of the Ivory Empress, broken off a small stone statue—maybe stolen, maybe purchased, the rest of the figure discarded.

The small, hunched being Vhek stared at in horror was like some terrible equivalent of the ancient and withered Mother Xo. Its inky, hairless frame was emaciated, though whether the bones that jutted through its skin corresponded to a human skeleton was uncertain. Viewing the creature, one might be reminded of an old and ailing black cat. It stood on its hind legs, further balanced by a long tapering tail, and gazed back at Vhek inscrutably with two human-like eyes that almost appeared to glow from within, though perhaps that was simply in contrast to its otherwise featureless face.

Vhek knew that this one was no ghost or lost soul. It was a corporeal, living thing.

"Don't!" screamed Sister Fuyen, who was the older of the two naked women.

Vhek was raising his gun to point at the creature, even as it took a step toward him, extending its arms.

As if startled by Sister Fuyen's cry, the room's shadows flinched. Vhek hadn't noticed before that the room's shadows seethed, churned, as if a restless audience of barely discernible figures had gathered around to witness the ritual that had been about to commence. *These* were the ghostly remnants…come to honor their living representative.

The First One stepped outside its painted circle, in doing so accidentally bumping the foremost brass bowl. The head of the Ivory Empress tumbled out onto the floor. The creature was frail and uncoordinated, but it still reached for Vhek's face with curled fingers.

Vhek fired into the First One's withered body, three times in rapid succession, at the same time that Captain Khieu—who had retrieved his service sidearm from his bundle of clothing—fired at Vhek.

"No!" cried Jee, charging past her brother and swinging her sword.

Before Khieu could turn his gun toward her, before he could even really register that she was rushing at him, Jee buried her blade deeply between his neck and shoulder. Khieu let out one hard liquid cough, stumbled back with the sword firmly wedged in his body. He fell against the wall, amidst the audience of hungry shadows.

Jee turned to see Vhek stumbling backward too. He collapsed, still holding his pistol.

From where he was slumped with his back propped against the wall, Khieu made a feeble attempt to raise his gun toward Vhek again, but it seemed too heavy. In any case, the shadows converged on him now, and his eyes went wide in horror as he realized they sought to feed on him.

"No, no, no!" Sister Fuyen wailed, kneeling beside the body of the First One where it had fallen just outside the painted ring. She tried to prop the scarecrow of a body up in her arms. She sobbed, "It was the last of its kind, do you understand? Do you monsters know what you've done? It was the *last* of the First Ones!"

Jee ignored her. She knelt by Vhek, who lay bleeding from the bullet wound in his chest. She put her hand over the wound, though there was no good to come from that except to hide it from her eyes. The blood pulsed between her fingers in any case.

"Oh, Vhek!" she sobbed. "My brother! My *brother!*"

Vhek rolled his head to watch Sister Fuyen cradle the dead First One. Even as he looked that way, he saw its body—barely substantial already—was liquifying, reduced to an almost gelatinous mass in her arms. Already its limbs were gone, and human-like eyes could no longer be discerned in its empty face.

"You are surely the children of that bitch the Ivory Empress!" Sister Fuyen screeched. "It wasn't enough that she abandoned her first offspring…she had to send *you* to kill the last of them too! You heartless *assassins!* You're worse than any demon in the Ten Hells!" She looked up from the mass of rot in her arms, her crazed eyes meeting Vhek's, then Jee's. "It lived in this house for *decades*—trapped for its own protection when it yearned to be free! And sometimes it got free, and you wanted to kill it that day in the river, but it always came back here where we could honor it the way it deserved! Poor, ancient thing...so lonely...so hungry...watching the outside world without comprehension because it had the mind of a child! Don't you see? It was just an eternal *child!*"

With the First One's final residue sloughing off her lap, Sister Fuyen lurched to her feet and went to Captain Khieu, who was now dead, with perhaps the last dregs of his life's essence sucked out of him. She bent to take the pistol from his hand.

Vhek lifted his gun a little off the floor and fired one shot at the nun. As she turned, she seemed to see the bullet as it flew at her. It struck her in the forehead, splitting the back of her shaven head. She dropped heavily onto Khieu's body.

All this time, the bartender had passively bent double with his fingers laced across his head, and the bar girl had shrunk down in a corner, covering her head with her arms. Madly, she seemed to be both cackling and sobbing at the same time.

Pan-Koy appeared in the room, gun held ready. He saw Vhek lying there.

"Call an ambulance!" Jee cried.

The policeman snapped his gaze about the room. He saw his captain and Sister Fuyen dead in a weirdly sexual tangle. The submissive bartender, the bar girl cowering in the corner. But there was nothing left of the last of the First Ones, and with it had dissipated the audience of hungry shadows.

Then Pan-Koy got out his cell phone, making a call for the town's single ambulance, while Kwen entered the room holding her sword blade against the throat of her terrified captive, who had learned how to breathe again.

Vhek let go of his handgun. He reached up to Jee, who crouched over him with her tears falling on his neck. He placed his hand on her back, ran his palm down and then up again, down and up. He smiled at her wordlessly, and Jee understood what he was doing. For the last time, as when she had requested it of him as a child, he was rubbing her back. And then the life went from his eyes.

At the same time, at the temple of the Ivory Empress on its little island, Mother Xo drew her last breath.

The town's police, led by Captain Pan-Koy, knew better than to try to stop the nuns of the Order of the Ivory Empress from swarming into the building that had housed the bar to perform their rites of exorcism. This, despite the fact that these rites included setting fire to the room in which the Last Ones had performed their ceremonies to summon the ghosts of the First Ones so that they might feed upon human hosts in this town, and in so doing—at least, according to the nuns' speculation—transfer the life force they gathered to their one living member to keep it alive.

The nuns had also speculated that the Last Ones had escalated their ceremonies of late to coincide with the imminent death of Mother Xo, and her anticipated replacement by Sister Fuyen. In years past, perhaps the First Ones had been prevented from feasting so openly because Mother Xo's presence had been too strong, and had blocked them either consciously—through her appeals to the Ivory Empress for the protection of her worshippers—or even unconsciously, for the many long years she had lived.

In any case, Captain Pan-Koy and his men could do little more than oversee the raid, focusing their efforts on keeping back the crowd of townspeople that had gathered to watch, and making sure the fires within didn't spread to neighboring buildings.

*   *   *

Mother Kwen allowed Sister Jee to conduct a service to honor her brother's memory at the temple of the Ivory Empress, where lately it had become necessary for the ferry to add some runs to its schedule. The other temples had seen an increase in attendance as well, as the townspeople prayed that the First Ones would never return to make this town their hunting ground, or a place for vengeance.

At the service she herself had conducted earlier, to honor the passing of Mother Xo, Mother Kwen had asked for the Ivory Empress to have pity on her original progeny, and help them find the peace they had never known, even if that peace was only nothingness.

One of the townspeople, a stonemason who specialized in producing gravestones for the town's cemetery, where Vhek's ashes would be interred, had fashioned four new spheres to replace those that had been stolen from the statue of the Ivory Empress, the lotus-shaped pedestal of which was presently buried under heaped flower arrangements brought by worshippers.

The service for Lieutenant Vhek was held in the temple's shrine hall, of course, where more flower arrangements crowded about the altar. An official police portrait of Vhek had been blown up to poster size and stood at the altar beside the ceramic vase that held his ashes.

During her service for her brother, Jee reverently lifted the vase of ash and held it against her body with one arm as those assembled watched, including a number of fellow police officers from the capital city of Haikan, among them Vhek's captain. Jee removed the vase's lid and set it down, then carried the vase to Vhek's two young sons, who stood close by. Jee pressed her finger into the ashes, then smudged the oldest boy's forehead. She repeated this process with the younger child. While doing so, she smiled down into their tearful upturned faces serenely, like the Ivory Empress herself, doing her best to keep the tears from her own eyes. For now, at least…until she was in her private quarters again.

Jee nodded politely to Vhek's solemn widow before continuing on to two other guests: her mother, whom she hadn't seen in four years, and her new husband. Jee again pressed her finger into ash and dabbed her mother's forehead, somehow maintaining her serene smile despite witnessing her mother's weeping. Still cradling the vase, Jee then returned to the altar. Before replacing the vase's lid, she inserted her finger into the ash a final time, brought it up to her own forehead, and marked herself there.

Then, to conclude the services, speaking her prayer in a clear, strong voice for those assembled to hear—Mother Kwen and the rest of the nuns, Captain Pan-Koy and other members of the local police, and so many townspeople that their numbers overflowed the shrine hall into the open courtyard outside—Jee asked the Ivory Empress and the other nine Jeweled Gods to ensure that her beloved brother's passage to the Ten Heavens was a straight one, and that the gods take him into their arms with all their love.

ABOUT THE AUTHOR

Jeffrey Thomas's many books include the short story collection *Punktown* (Prime Books), and the novels *Deadstock* (Solaris Books), *Blue War* (Solaris Books), and *The American* (JournalStone). Other works in his "Unnamed Country" setting include the collection *The Unnamed Country* (Word Horde), the chapbook *Scenes from a Village* (Oddness), and the novella *The Spirit of Place* (Earthling Publications). Though Thomas considers Viet Nam his second home, he resides in Massachusetts.